Jeremy chuckled. "Is this the way it's going to be?"

"What?" With an indignant sniff, Taylor shot up out of her chair.

He caught her hand. "Us sparring back and forth continuously until you leave?"

She pushed him away, one hand flat against his chest. "I don't mind."

"I do."

"Jeremy…"

It was all he could do not to take her in his arms. "I'd like us to be friends again."

Surveying him with exaggerated politeness, she crossed her arms in front of her. "Seriously?"

"Seriously." He stood slowly.

He had missed her. So much.

Dear Reader,

Is it just me, or has celebrity news gotten way out of control these days? I suppose it is one thing for the actual stars, who sign up for that kind of fishbowl existence. But what about the ordinary people around them—like you and me—who inadvertently find themselves in the midst of all the craziness?

Heroine Taylor O'Quinn is a novelist leading a normal life until the film rights to her first book are sold. Suddenly her book is being turned into a movie, and she is asked to write the screenplay. Happily, she agrees, and there the trouble starts. The next thing she knows her life is tabloid fodder, and none of what they are reporting is true!

Disillusioned and in need of sanctuary, Taylor heads for Laramie, Texas. It's no safer. Her unrequited love, Jeremy Carrigan, is there. He's never forgiven her for deserting him during their med school days. And he's never gotten over the secret crush he had for her, either. Physician, rancher, gentleman to the core—he decides he will protect her from the forces set on ruining her. But who will protect them from their hearts?

I hope you have as much fun reading this sexy romp as I did writing it, and I invite you to visit www.cathygillenthacker.com.

Happy reading!

Cathy Gillen Thacker

Cathy Gillen Thacker
THE GENTLEMAN RANCHER

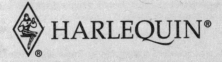

HARLEQUIN®

TORONTO • NEW YORK • LONDON
AMSTERDAM • PARIS • SYDNEY • HAMBURG
STOCKHOLM • ATHENS • TOKYO • MILAN • MADRID
PRAGUE • WARSAW • BUDAPEST • AUCKLAND

ISBN-13: 978-0-373-75205-8
ISBN-10:   0-373-75205-9

THE GENTLEMAN RANCHER

Printed in U.S.A.

ABOUT THE AUTHOR

Cathy Gillen Thacker married her high school sweetheart and hasn't had a dull moment since. Why? you ask. Well, there were three kids, various pets, any number of automobiles, several moves across the country, his and her careers and sundry other experiences (some of which were exciting and some of which weren't). But mostly, there was love and friendship and laughter, and lots of experiences she wouldn't trade for the world. Please visit her Web site at www.cathygillenthacker.com.

Books by Cathy Gillen Thacker

HARLEQUIN AMERICAN ROMANCE

  997—THE VIRGIN'S SECRET MARRIAGE*
1013—THE SECRET WEDDING WISH*
1022—THE SECRET SEDUCTION*
1029—PLAIN JANE'S SECRET LIFE*
1054—HER SECRET VALENTINE*
1080—THE ULTIMATE TEXAS BACHELOR**
1096—SANTA'S TEXAS LULLABY**
1112—A TEXAS WEDDING VOW**
1125—BLAME IT ON TEXAS**
1141—A LARAMIE, TEXAS CHRISTMAS**
1157—FROM TEXAS, WITH LOVE**
1169—THE RANCHER NEXT DOOR†
1181—THE RANCHER'S FAMILY THANKSGIVING†
1201—THE GENTLEMAN RANCHER†

  *The Brides of Holly Springs
 **The McCabes: Next Generation
 †Texas Legacies: The Carrigans

Chapter One

Trouble In Paradise?

Newlyweds Zak and Zoe Townsend may act like love-birds on their reality TV show, detailing the most intimate moments of their first two years as husband and wife, but on the set of their first feature film, *Sail Away*, the mood has been anything but romantic. The pop/rock stars have been at each other's throats since filming began two months ago. Why, no one seems to know, least of all the legions of fans who have rooted for the Hollywood couple since their fairytale romance began...

June 1 edition, *Celebrities Weekly* magazine

As the sun went down, bringing dusk to the West Texas sky, Taylor O'Quinn had been in her Jeep Liberty for seventeen hours and fifty-three minutes. By her calculations, she had about twenty more minutes to go before arriving at the Chamberlain ranch, outside of Laramie, Texas. She couldn't get there a moment too soon.

Her air-conditioning had begun malfunctioning somewhere near the California-Arizona border. By the time she reached

New Mexico, it had quit altogether. Driving with the windows down hadn't been so bad when she was up in the mountains, but when she had hit the flatlands of Texas, the heat had been brutal.

One-hundred-and-ten degree summer heat—even when blowing over her body at sixty-five miles an hour, was still hotter than blazes. The only thing keeping her going was the thought of the swimming pool awaiting her. Well, that and the fact that she had a place to stay rent-free for the next few weeks. Another fringe benefit was no one would ever think to look for her at the family home of her best friend.

Speaking of which… Taylor pulled over long enough to loop the hands-free receiver over her ear and dial her cell.

Paige Chamberlain answered on the third ring. "Hey, girl-friend, where are you?"

Her familiar voice brought a smile to Taylor's face. "About fifteen minutes away, I think."

"Great!" Paige exuded her customary good cheer and stellar organizational skills. "I left a key for you in the planter next to the door. Help yourself to anything in the fridge. The yellow guest room in the main house is yours. Clean towels are in the linen closet across from the hall bath." After a brief interruption, she returned to the line. "I've got an appendec-tomy to do, so I'll be at the hospital a few more hours. Until then, make yourself at home."

"I will. And thanks, Paige."

The sound of an announcement over the hospital intercom system blared in the background. "No problem." Paige shouted to be heard above it. "See you soon!"

Taylor said goodbye and concentrated on finding the un-assuming entrance to the ranch, a task that was not so easy as dusk covered the Texas countryside with a soft gray gloom. Luckily, the plain black wrought-iron archway, sans lettering of any kind, was just as Taylor remembered it. She turned down the single blacktop lane and drove through unkempt fields of mesquite and scrub brush that remained wild until she was completely out of sight of the two-lane farm-to-market road. Then, the fence started, the grass grew more manicured, and the sprawling hacienda-style ranch house rose above the plain, glowing with welcoming lights. The personal retreat was an oasis of privacy and rustic comfort, the kind of home where legendary actor-film director Beau Chamberlain and his movie-critic wife, Dani, could live in relative anonymity. Taylor had stayed there many times when she and Paige had been college—and med school—roommates.

Acutely aware of just how long ago that had been—a good seven plus years—Taylor parked in the empty driveway and got out. Leaving her belongings in the car, she passed the front of the house and followed the flagstone path to the backyard. The pool was designed to look like a hidden lagoon, complete with waterfall and tropical plants. The underwater lights weren't on, but there was enough illumination from the adjacent ranch house and the guesthouse on the opposite side to allow Taylor to take a swim.

The shimmering blue water beckoned, cool and inviting.

Deciding to heck with going back to search for her swimsuit—she had waited far too long for relief from the searing summer heat as it was—Taylor kicked off her sandals and reached for the hem of her sweat-sticky T-shirt. Suddenly a familiar masculine voice jolted her from the task at hand.

"I wouldn't, if I were you."

IT FIGURED, Jeremy Carrigan thought, that the first time he'd gone skinny-dipping in years, he'd get caught with his pants off. By none other than the most aggravating woman he had ever had the misfortune to meet in his life.

Taylor O'Quinn turned to get a closer look.

In profile, she'd been beautiful.

Facing him, she was even lovelier. In the years since he'd seen her, the delicate bone structure of her facial features had only become more pronounced. Long-lashed blue eyes dominated a slender nose and full, soft lips. As she released her thick black hair from the elastic band that had been holding it away from her face, the windswept strands fell, rippling across her slender shoulders and brushing at the graceful slope of her neck. Lower still the perfection continued in her five-foot-six form. His pulse picked up as his glance roved her full breasts, slender waist, curvy hips and long, shapely legs.

Somehow, Jeremy thought, it wasn't all that surprising to find that Taylor O'Quinn had only gotten sexier as she aged. What stunned him was the realization that, even after all these years of resentful silence, he still wanted her as much as ever.

Taylor froze—as if sensing she were being scrutinized. Slowly, she peered into the shadowy cove where he was lounging. When she spied him, her chin took on the familiar tilt. "What are you doing here?" Taylor demanded.

Jeremy put up a staying hand to keep her from coming any closer. "I might ask the same question of you," he remarked dryly, silently wishing his response to her would fade.

"Paige said I could stay here with her for a few weeks, while her own house is being remodeled and her parents are in Montana. She didn't say anything about you being here."

Jeremy shrugged. "She didn't tell me anything about you arriving, either."

Still a good twenty-five feet away from him, Taylor knelt to test the temperature of the water with her hand. "Then you're just here to swim?" She regarded him with lifted brows.

The way she'd said that told Jeremy she wasn't here just to get in a workout, either. Which probably meant Paige had neglected to tell them both something very important. He pushed aside his irritation with effort. He shrugged matter-of-factly. "I'm bunking here for a few weeks."

Taylor took her wet hand and rubbed it across the back of her neck, in a futile effort, he guessed, to cool down. The gold shamrock necklace she had been given by her late grandmother, and wore as a symbol of luck and blessing, still glistened around her neck. "In the guesthouse," she presumed, obviously hoping to put as much physical distance between them as possible.

"Paige has the guesthouse," Jeremy corrected, treading water, and drifting further back into a shadowy corner so he could still gaze at her, but she could not see much of him. "I have the green bedroom in the main house."

Taylor approached the corner of the pool, caddy-corner to him, where the steps were located. Hand on the railing, she walked down until the water came up to the hem of her capris. "Don't you have your own place?" She sounded piqued.

He couldn't blame her, they hadn't parted well. And they hadn't communicated with each other in the seven years since. "As a matter of fact, I do own a home." His voice resonated with pride. "Lago Vista Ranch, on Lake Laramie."

She walked back up the steps, to the decorative tile edging the swimming pool. Standing there, running her foot across the surface of the water, she seemed to be weighing her next move. Ever so slowly, she directed her glance at him. "Then why aren't you staying there?"

Jeremy wished people would stop asking him that. It was all he'd heard for the past two years. He let his shoulders rise and fall. "It doesn't have any indoor plumbing at the moment."

She strode toward Jeremy and looked at him as if he were an idiot. "You bought a place with no working plumbing?" Disbelief resonated in her low tone.

"I figured I'd get the septic tank replaced eventually and in the meantime it has...portable...accommodations for emergencies."

"You have a port-a-potty on your property?"

"It was either that or build an outhouse. This seemed more practical."

"I'll bet." She edged closer still. She seemed to be regarding him with the same fascination she would have shown an unfamiliar species in the Houston zoo. "Just out of curiosity...what was the deal-maker on the property?"

That, Jeremy thought, was easy. He gestured expansively. "It had to be a ranch and it had to have a water view."

Taylor chewed on her lower lip. "I get the wanting to live on the water thing."

Jeremy wasn't surprised. Water had always soothed Taylor as much as it relaxed him.

"I don't get the ranch." She peered at him through narrowed lashes. "You've never been a cowboy."

Nor did he intend to raise cattle, horses or any other form of livestock. He angled his thumb at the center of his chest. "I'm a *gentleman* rancher. And I wanted acreage around whatever home I purchased for privacy reasons."

She tilted her head, considering. "Does it have a pool?"

"It's got a dock...and private access to the lake," Jeremy related with pride.

Without warning, she looked down into the water and smirked. "Nice." She took her sweet time lifting her gaze to his. "What happened to your swim trunks?"

Jeremy grimaced, trying to ignore the way the blood was rushing to his lower half. All she'd have to do was look down again and she'd know exactly what was on his mind—at least subconsciously.

"They're in the house." He kept his voice casual, his eyes

on hers. He smiled slowly, offering, "If you want to go and get them for me…"

Contrary as ever, Taylor replied, "Can't say as I do." Hips swaying lightly, she sauntered back to the opposite side of the pool, began emptying the pockets on her capri pants. She set lipstick, keys, a receipt or two, and some change down on a glass-topped patio table. Jeremy's throat went dry at the thought of her stripped down, too. He cleared his throat, regarding her steadily. "Tell me you're not doing what I think you're doing."

Amusement rippled in her voice. "What do you think I'm doing?"

He flashed her a cryptic smile. "Taking off your clothes."

"Brilliant deduction, Sherlock."

Treading water—naked—while she was standing up there, observing him, was tough enough. Having her in the pool with him… A chill of intense awareness rippled through him. "You don't want to do this," he insisted.

She smirked again, not the least bit dissuaded. "You only think that because you don't have a clue how hot I am."

Once again, Taylor O'Quinn was dead wrong. He had always known how sexy she was. It just hadn't been a good idea, getting romantically involved with another first-year med school classmate.

He played it safe. Noncommittal. "I'm serious, Taylor."

She chose to ignore the unsubtle hint. "So am I." She lifted her arms above her head and engaged in a languid whole-body stretch. "If the sight of a naked woman bothers you—and it really shouldn't, given how many years you've been a doctor now—then turn your back."

And miss the show? No way!

He studied her, not believing she would really stand there and strip in front of him.

Then again, with the swiftness with which her capris and T-shirt had just come off… Clad only in a pale pink bra and panties that revealed a hell of a lot more than they covered, she reached around behind her.

Blood surged, low and fast. It wasn't that he was unfamiliar with what she was about to uncover. In medical school, they'd had to practice giving other students physicals, before they examined any real patients. Jeremy and Taylor had been in the same Introduction To Clinical Medicine section. Hence, they'd both seen each other and eight other fellow students in states of undress. The experience had been humbling and instructional. It hadn't been arousing—they'd been learning the art of being a doctor.

This was different. This was no classroom setting. He wasn't in doctor mode. Nor was she…

He swore, then reluctantly gave her the privacy she deserved and turned his head.

Seconds later, the water splashed with the force of a clean, graceful dive. She swam along the bottom of the pool and came up, on the opposite side.

TAYLOR WATCHED Jeremy's eyes widen as her shoulders broke the surface and he focused on the bra straps clinging to her. She couldn't help it, she started to laugh.

She waggled her eyebrows at him. "Faked you out, didn't I?"

"It would seem I'm the only one at a disadvantage, here."

And Taylor wished like heck he wasn't.

Seeing Jeremy's buff body, even through the soft illumination of patio lamps and the filter of water, was a jolt to her system. Six foot two and muscled…everywhere. His broad shoulders and long limbs were all male, and imposing enough to make her feel out of her depth here. His hair was a very dark brown with the barest hint of red. These days the damp strands were on the short side, maybe an inch and a half long, and styled in the cut so popular with professional guys his age. But there was nothing usual about the high cheekbones and eloquent brow of his angular face. A blunt masculine nose topped an even more rugged jaw and the don't-toy-with-me set of his lips.

She'd always been attracted to him physically, even when she couldn't say they respected each other very much. Unbidden, the memory of the last time they had seen each other and the harsh words they had exchanged, returned.

"You're making a mistake, Taylor. Don't do it... Don't quit!"

Disillusionment filtered through her at the memory of that angst-ridden time in her life.

Jeremy swam closer. "I guess this is the point where I congratulate you on your success as an author."

It shouldn't have mattered to her what Jeremy Carrigan thought. Any more than she cared about what her parents or her two surgeon-brothers thought of her career choice. To her chagrin, it still did. Taylor turned her gaze from the water beading on his sinewy shoulders. Struggling to ignore her reaction to his nearness, she sidestroked a short distance away. "You heard?"

Still treading water, Jeremy looked her square in the eye. "That The Guy Who Sailed Away and the Girl Who Found Herself is being turned into a movie starring Zoe and Zak Townsend?" He shoved a hand through his waterlogged hair. "It would have been hard not to know that, given how much it's been in the news for the last six months."

"The celebrity and entertainment news."

"That's still news." He regarded her through squinted eyes. "So what's next? Are you going to move out to Hollywood for good now? Write more books? More screenplays?"

She noted he didn't seem to want her to do that now any more than he ever had. "No."

"How come?"

She breast-stroked down to the opposite end of the pool and sat down on the lowest of the circular steps, so the majority of her body was covered by the soothing chill of the water. "I prefer writing novels to movie scripts."

"Meaning what?" He studied her, a thoughtful expression on his handsome face. "If they turn your next novel into a movie, you won't write that screenplay, too?"

About this much, Taylor was certain. "I'm not selling the movie rights to another book."

He swam closer. His glance took in the new stiffness of her spine. "How come?" he asked.

"I—" Taylor abruptly turned her glance, to avoid getting a full-on view of everything about him she had sought to forget. Suddenly she saw movement in the hedge of red-tipped photinia bushes enclosing the landscaped backyard. "What the…?" She frowned, as a branch snapped, close to the ground. Leaves rustled.

Jeremy's gaze narrowed, too. He tensed. "You hear that?" he asked.

Taylor nodded.

"Could be some form of wildlife," Jeremy speculated.

But what kind? Taylor wondered. Armadillos and porcupines usually had more sense than to wander this close to the ranch house. Snakes, on the other hand, had been known to search out water in the summer heat. More than a few had ended up in Texas swimming pools…surprising the heck out of the people in or around them.

Jeremy swam closer. "You stay here. I'm going to check it out."

His insistence on being chivalrous now—when he had not done so during the time when she desperately needed and wanted his support—rankled. "Don't be ridiculous." Taylor stood, dripping water onto the steps. Haughtily she announced, "I'll look."

Oblivious to his lack of clothing, Jeremy vaulted out of the water. He clamped a staying hand just above her elbow. "No. I'll go."

Ignoring the view of his gloriously handsome body, she wrested free and stalked in the direction of the sound. To her mounting frustration, it took Jeremy less than two strides to catch up. She increased her pace determinedly. So did he. Side by side, they cautiously approached the hedge.

As they closed in, a fifty-something woman, clad in outrageously short shorts and a halter top, shot up. Simultaneously, a camera flash went off in their eyes, temporarily blinding them. By the time they could focus again, she was already running away.

"Sorry!" she shouted sheepishly over her shoulder. "Didn't mean to get you. I was looking for Beau!"

"It HAPPENS every once in a great while," Paige Chamberlain said, upon arriving home an hour later.

As always, the tall, lanky redhead looked just as apt to step off the cover of a magazine as out of an operating room. Although that wasn't surprising to Taylor, given the glamorous yet down-to-earth couple Paige claimed as parents. Dani and Beau Chamberlain were both gorgeous and upstanding members of the entertainment industry. Beau came at it from an actor/director position, Dani the publishing side as a renowned movie critic. Taylor had admired both long before she'd met them, when she and Paige had become friends during college.

In turn, Paige had admired Taylor's parents' talent for surgery and had spent many hours discussing the pros and cons of each surgical specialty with them. Taylor's dad, of course, had favored neurosurgery, his specialty. Her mom had pushed for a specialization in the cardio-thoracic field. Instead, Paige had followed her own path and ended up specializing in pediatric surgery.

"So it doesn't bother you then?" Taylor asked skeptically.

"It's par for the course," Paige said. "We get some fan lurking behind the hedges, trying to get a photo of my dad. If you see her again, we'll call the sheriff's department, but she was probably harmless. Just out of curiosity," Paige opened the fridge and withdrew three bottles of beer, "why didn't you two just get her camera and take the film away?"

Jeremy looked at Taylor. Not about to reveal their state of undress at the time, Taylor busied herself making hamburgers for the three of them.

"Never got close enough to her." Jeremy apparently agreed with Taylor that no one save the two of them, and the interloper, need know about their stripped-down appearance. "The woman hopped on a motorbike—hidden behind the bushes—and took off. It didn't seem worth giving chase."

"Probably wasn't." Paige sighed.

"Speaking of the unexpected," Jeremy continued.

Taylor nodded. She and Jeremy didn't agree on much but they did agree on this. She turned to face their mutual friend. "Why didn't you tell me Jeremy was already bunking here?"

Paige shrugged. "Because it shouldn't make any difference. The ranch is plenty big enough for the three of us. Especially since Jeremy and I both will be working at the hospital the majority of the time. Furthermore, I don't have any problem saying I am getting pretty tired of being in the middle of your quarrel."

"Hey," Jeremy interrupted with a scowl, "we never asked you to take sides."

"Right," Paige drawled. "You just stopped speaking to

each other and forbid me to speak about either of you to the other. Not cool."

Taylor glared at Jeremy.

Jeremy glared back.

"It's time the two of you made up so the three of us can be friends again, the way we used to be." Paige munched on a potato chip. "I miss the fun we used to have, you know?"

Taylor slid the patties into a sizzling skillet and went to the sink to wash her hands. "Even if we bury the hatchet, it is never going to be the same. You two are still in medicine. I'm not."

"You could be again if you wanted to be." Jeremy rummaged through the fridge.

Paige looked reprovingly at Jeremy, as if to say, "Not that old argument again!"

"My sentiments exactly," Taylor said.

Jeremy tossed them a look over his shoulder. He set pickles, mustard, ketchup and mayo on the counter. "I can't help feeling the way I do." He straightened and shut the door.

"Yes," Paige countered, stepping past him to get the lettuce, tomato and cheese, "but you can certainly help saying it."

Jeremy harrumphed at Taylor. "You were the most talented student in our class."

Taylor flipped the burgers. "Grades aren't everything, Carrigan."

He lounged against the counter opposite her, arms folded across his chest. "You had a way with patients."

Trying not to think what his steady appraisal and deep voice did to her, Taylor appraised him right back. "There are many professions that require good people skills."

Cynicism lifted one corner of his mouth. "You shouldn't have quit just because your parents expected you to be a doctor."

With effort, Taylor tamped down her rising temper. "I quit because I wanted to write."

"You could write and still be a doctor."

Taylor looked at Paige. "Make him shut up or I'm going to deck him."

Paige layered sliced tomatoes on the platter, next to the lettuce and onions. "You heard the woman." She sent Jeremy a debilitating look. "Shut. Up."

Jeremy moved so he could see around Paige. "Go ahead and punch me," he dared Taylor. "I'm just saying what has to be said."

"No." Taylor closed the distance between them in three quick strides. She tapped his chest. "You're saying what *you* feel. Your emotions have nothing to do with what *I* want or need."

"Probably not," he acknowledged. "I just think it's a shame. The world needs more doctors like you—"

Paige put two fingers between her teeth and whistled loud enough to stop traffic on Times Square. "Enough!" She waved her arms like a referee breaking up a fight. "Both of you—apologize—now!"

"For what?" Jeremy and Taylor said in unison.

Rolling her eyes, Paige touched her fingers to her forehead. "I give up. I'm going to the guesthouse."

"Don't you want your burger?" Taylor slid the sizzling meat onto an open bun.

"Don't mind if I do." In stormy silence, Paige added condiments to her sandwich and a handful of chips. She took her plate and bottle of beer with her, calling over her shoulder, "Good night!"

Silence fell.

Taylor added the works to her burger, too. "I think I'll eat in my room."

Jeremy clamped a hand on her shoulder, delaying her exit with a sincere look. "I'm sorry. I shouldn't have said that. Again."

His apology seemed genuine enough, Taylor noted grudgingly. She set her plate on the kitchen table, next to her beverage, and took a seat. She spread her napkin over her lap. "The real question is, are you going to bring it up again?"

"No." Jeremy garnished his burger, then sat at the other end of the table. He sat down and dug in. "Especially since it's obvious I'd be wasting my breath."

They ate in silence for several minutes.

Aware she had waited years for the chance to go toe-to-toe with him over this very subject, she said, "It's not as if I never sold a book, you know. I'm a published novelist and a screenwriter." She didn't know why she felt she had to keep saying that. If she'd been a doctor, she wouldn't have been forced to defend the value of her profession. Of course, if she'd been a doctor, people wouldn't have questioned the value of her job.

He polished off one burger, got up to get another. "Got any copies of your book with you?"

Her defenses snapped back into place. "No."

He grabbed another handful of chips, too. "I'd like to read it."

Was this a trick? Another way to continue his crusade to get her back into medicine? It didn't appear so. More like a way to assuage his guilt. She didn't need penance from him, either. She made no effort to hide her irritation. "You don't have to do that."

"Why don't you want me to?" he asked, even more curious. He kicked back in his chair and polished off his beer. "I thought all authors wanted to have their stuff read. Isn't that the point of being a novelist? To be popular? To have your voice heard and all that?"

Maybe for some. She wrote because she had to, because she had something to say, stories to tell that wouldn't get out of her head until they were written down. Taylor'd been a storyteller as far back as she could remember, always drifting off into daydreams and conjuring up movies in her head. It was a heaven-sent gift that was as much a part of her as her straight black hair, and just as impossible to explain.

She sighed and looked Jeremy in the eye. "The only reason I would want you to read my book is because you enjoy that type of story. Since I can't really see you ever picking up a chick lit novel by anyone else—to read for pleasure—then the answer is a resounding no. Do not do me any favors!"

Merriment crept into his dark brown eyes. "I could broaden my horizons."

Taylor snorted and kicked back in her chair, too. "I'm not saying you don't need to do that."

"But?" Electricity sparked between them.

She shook her head, aware her heart was racing. "Not at my expense."

His handsome features tightened into a mock-reproving look. "You're awfully prickly."

"You're awfully pushy," she retorted.

"And moody."

"Keep it up, I dare you."

His grin broadened. "So what's really going on with your life?"

Taylor jumped up to clear the table. "What do you mean?"

His movements as lazy as hers were restless, he got up to help. "You told Paige you drove eighteen hours straight to get here, when you could have taken a flight and had your Jeep shipped back to—where was it you said you'd been living?"

"Chesapeake, Virginia." Taylor slid dishes into the dishwasher, straightened, all attitude once again. "What's your point?"

"My point is," he explained, his voice as silky-smooth as hers was blunt and impatient, "that you told Paige the move back home could have been done for you, at movie studio expense, if you had been willing to wait another few weeks for it all to be arranged, by their business affairs office. Instead, you got in your car and drove all the way here, on very little notice."

He was far too observant for comfort. Worse, he'd always seen things that no one else noticed. She tilted her chin at him. "So?"

Jeremy stared at her with a steely resolve that matched her own. "The last time you took off in your Jeep—that I know of anyway—and drove that long and that hard, was the day you quit med school." He paused, his gaze roaming the contours of her face, lingering on her lips, before slowly returning to her eyes. "So what's happening in your life that Paige and I don't know about?" he asked, even more softly. "What are you running from this time?"

Chapter Two

"And Last But Not Least," Anchor Mandy Stone read the teleprompter with a salacious smile, "up and coming novelist-turned-screenwriter Taylor O'Quinn set tongues to wagging when she skipped the wrap party for *Sail Away*. Insiders were not surprised. Dozens of rewrites for the troubled pic have left everyone feeling frustrated and unhappy—including the film's two leads, Zak and Zoe Townsend."

(Cut to film of wrap party.)

"The story had some problems, as it was originally written," Zak admitted, presenting his best side to the camera and taking his wife's hand.

"But we've done our best to fix them," Zoe added, pausing earnestly.

"We just hope Taylor's all right." Zak wrapped an arm around Zoe's shoulders and pulled Zoe in close to his side.

Zoe nodded, looking even more doe-eyed and distressed. "When Taylor left the set, and drove off in her SUV, she was in tears…"

June 2 edition of *Short-takes*!
Celebrity Entertainment Network

Taylor couldn't help feeling relieved when their heated confrontation was interrupted by Jeremy's pager. As he put in a call to his answering service, she scrambled to come up with a reasonable response to his accusation. Unfortunately, her reprieve was short-lived.

Medical crisis averted, Jeremy snapped his cell phone shut and gazed at her expectantly. "Well? What do you have to say for yourself?"

Taylor set the damp dishcloth down with more than necessary care. She turned back to Jeremy, her expression stoic. "I'm not running away." She enunciated each word distinctly, then moved past him.

Arms folded, Jeremy watched her head for the exit. Her actions evoked bittersweet memories of a time when they could have had everything. If only she had stayed in Texas, instead of heading off for parts unknown… "Then why are you bolting the kitchen?"

As she whirled back around to face him, her long black hair rippled across her shoulders. "Perhaps because I'm done talking to you?" She smiled sweetly.

Jeremy shook his head. "You're running from me the way you ran from whatever's going on in Los Angeles."

Defiance gleamed in her blue eyes. "You're wrong."

"I don't think so." He closed the distance between them. "I've always been able to read you like a book."

Temper flared in her cheeks, turning them a rosy pink. "Then you know how ticked off you're making me right now."

"It doesn't change the truth," he drawled.

"I'm going to bed." She glared at him.

He glared right back. "I'll still be here tomorrow."

She breathed in deeply and appeared to be counting backwards from…one thousand. "Hopefully you'll be at the hospital by the time I wake up," she predicted.

Aware he had gotten under her skin as quickly as always, he straightened. "Then I'll be here tomorrow night."

"Like Paige said, it's a big ranch house." She propped her hands on her slender hips. "We can coexist without actually coming in contact with each other."

Her heart was beating much too quickly—he could tell by the pulse in her throat. He twisted his lips into a crooked line then murmured, "That's not what Paige said."

"It's what I inferred," Taylor huffed.

Jeremy strolled closer, trying not to notice how quickly his body was responding to her. "You didn't let me help you the last time you were in trouble," he reminded her, making no effort to mask his frustration.

She stomped out the back door, through the screened porch. The door banged behind her. "That's because you weren't interested in helping me—you were trying to tell me what to do, think and feel, and I had enough of that from my family!"

Jeremy followed her across the decorative stones of the patio, toward the driveway. "You're right. My behavior was bad." He caught up with her next to her red Jeep. "It doesn't mean I can't make up for it now."

Taylor lifted the cargo door in stormy silence. The back was crammed with belongings, everything from dishes to lamps to computer, to clothes. Lots and lots of clothes, Jeremy noted.

"Why would you want to do that?" she demanded.

Because of the way you looked when you came up out of the water. Because I missed you. Because no one has ever made me feel the way you do when we go toe-to-toe like this.

Jeremy watched her sift through to the large suitcase on the very bottom. She grabbed hold of it and tried to ease it out. The weight on top of it kept it from budging. She yanked all the harder.

He brushed her aside with his body, and accomplished with ease what she had failed to do. Ignoring the scowl on her pretty face, he set the suitcase on the pavement. "I like challenges."

Muttering under her breath, she rummaged around until she was able to extract her laptop computer case, which had been wedged between two stacks of linens. The action caused the towels to slide toward her. Once again, Jeremy reached in quickly, catching the towels with one hand and steadying her by placing his other hand beneath her elbow.

She stumbled, regained her footing, and jerked free of him without so much as a thank you. "I'm not one of your family practice patients."

Thank heavens for small favors, because if she was, he'd have to keep his distance from her emotionally for ethical reasons. He paused, furrowing his brow. "How did you know what my specialty was?"

She turned her gaze to the sky. "I think Paige might have mentioned it one hundred thousand times."

He watched as she stood on tiptoe to catch and close the cargo door. "You remembered."

She pushed a button near the suitcase handle and yanked on the retractable grip. "Hard not to, when something is repeated that often." She waited until she heard the handle lock into place, then shifted the weight so the wheels were at an angle and hence able to easily roll. "And as long as we're being honest…"

"Yeah?"

Ducking his attempts to help her, she struggled to manage the laptop sliding down one shoulder, without stopping her forward progress. "Why are you suddenly hitting on me?"

He reached forward to wrest the bulky suitcase from her, despite her obvious wish he wouldn't. "You think that's what I'm doing?"

Reluctantly, she let him help her. With a toss of her head, she marched forward. "I don't know what you're doing," she called over her shoulders. "Except I am not one of those damsels in distress you are always dating, and then sending on their merry way when their crisis is over."

Jeremy winced as she held the door. "How do you know about that?"

"Paige," they said in unison.

He eased past, careful not to get her suitcase tangled up with the laptop case swinging off her shoulder. "I was just friends with all those women," he said, striding back toward the bedroom wing.

"Unlike Imogen Tate?"

Jeremy tensed. "You know about that?"

"I know you dated her for two years, starting right after I left Texas, and asked her to marry you. Instead of saying yes, she dumped you for a professional hockey player…and you've been on the rebound ever since."

Just because he couldn't seem to find a woman who came close to the one standing in front of him did not mean he was on the rebound. The truth was, he realized now, he and Imogen had embarked on a relationship that met their physical needs yet never placed any emotional demands on either of them. They were solo operators, each going their own way, never connecting for anything more than sex and social convenience. The few times he'd tried to help Imogen with her problems or have her listen to his had been a complete bust. But figuring Taylor did not need to know any of that, he shifted the attention back to her. "What do you know about rebound?"

He stood in the wing that housed the guest bedrooms, waiting for her to pick one. She noticed his belongings in the first bedroom and headed all the way down to the opposite end of the hall.

Her know-it-all smirk harkened back to their med school days. "If you have to ask me that, it shows how little you understand about me."

Suitcase in tow, he trailed behind her. "Uh-huh. Well, I know this. I know you didn't waste any time in the romance department after leaving Texas." He paused in the doorway of the suite she'd chosen. "How long did it take you to hook up with Baywatch Bart?"

"His name was Bartholomew Wyndham."

Aware he was sounding a little jealous, Jeremy continued in a more nonchalant tone, "I saw his picture. Who poses on the deck of a yacht?"

Taylor snatched her suitcase from him and rolled it toward the walk-in closet. "A guy who runs Bart's Charter Fishing Tours, perhaps?"

"Why'd you break up?" Was Taylor still carrying a torch for the guy?

Taylor set her laptop case next to the reading chair. "None of your business."

Had he hurt her? Was that why she was so...defensive?

Figuring it wouldn't hurt if they spent a little more time together, Jeremy came closer. "Why'd you get together?"

"Also. None. Of. Your. Business!" Taylor went back to her suitcase.

Jeremy watched her bend over to unzip it. "Find any more beach bums in Hollywood land?"

She extracted a toiletries bag and carried it into the adjoining bathroom. With the same ease she'd exhibited when they'd been med students, sharing a house with half a dozen other students of both sexes, she took out the facial cleanser and began to lather up her face. "I haven't been dating anyone for the last two years." Finished, she reached for a towel.

"How come?"

Briefly, she buried her face in the soft yellow terry cloth. "If you know so much about me, why don't you know that too?" Taylor left the bathroom and began to rifle through the suitcase.

She gave him a look that said, "If you don't mind…"

Taking the hint, he lifted a hand and eased out of the room. She shut the door behind him with a definite thud. Jeremy exhaled in frustration, then walked out the rear of the house, across the pool area to the guesthouse.

Paige's light was still on. She answered his knock with a look of aggravation. Open book to her chest, she waved him in. "That didn't take long."

He sank into a club chair in front of the fireplace and stretched his legs out in front of him. "What didn't take long?"

Paige settled on the far end of the sofa. "For the two of you to have a fight."

Jeremy shoved his hands in the pockets of his cargo shorts and studied the Remington painting above the mantle. "What makes you think we quarreled?"

"That look on your face," Paige said. "The one that says you still can't figure out what's really going on between the two of you."

Not true. They all knew that Taylor brought out the worst in him—the overbearing, intensely protective, got-to-have-the-last-word side his three sisters detested.

"We actively dislike one another," Jeremy observed dryly.

"There's that," Paige conceded with a dip of her head.

Jeremy had an idea where this was going. He stood and restlessly, began to pace. Eventually, he slanted his old friend a reproving look. "That's all there is."

Paige tried not to grin but failed miserably. "If you say so." She stuck her nose back in her book.

Jeremy scowled and continued to roam the living area. Given the amount of swimming he'd done earlier this evening, before Taylor had showed up, he should be relaxed. Instead, he was more tied up in knots than ever. In need of… hell, he didn't know what he needed…that was the problem. Aware Paige was still watching him with a twinkle in her eyes, he chided gruffly, "I didn't come over here so you could play shrink."

Paige sobered, for reasons all her own. "Then why *did* you come over here?"

As long as he was here, he might as well ask. He'd wasted enough of Paige's time already. Jeremy massaged the rigid muscles along the back of his neck. "Do you have a copy of Taylor's book?"

"Yes, I do, and it's back at my house—in town—nicely packed away so it won't be damaged by all the renovation currently going on there."

Jeremy swore beneath his breath.

Paige lifted her brow. "You really want to read it that badly, hmm?"

"I thought I might browse through a chapter or two," Jeremy allowed, casually.

Paige considered that, coming to some private conclusion he would just as soon not know about, then eventually said, "There's a signed copy in my mother's office. It's on the shelf next to her desk. You can read that if you promise to put it back. Anything happens to it," she paused, accompanying her warning with a stern look, "my mother will have your head. She says it's one of the best chick lit novels she's ever read."

Jeremy'd heard that a lot in passing. He'd never ventured even a glimpse of anything Taylor had written. "What do you think?"

Paige turned sincere. "I share my mom's opinion. Taylor's really talented." She lifted a hand. "I don't know what the problem in her life is now—"

"You think there's something wrong now, too?" Jeremy interrupted.

"Duh. She only drove eighteen hours to get here today. She wouldn't have done that if she weren't running from something."

Jeremy's mouth tightened. "My thoughts exactly."

"I offered her safe harbor here—as long as she needs. You mess with that, you wreck her peace of mind any more than it's been wrecked, and you're out of here."

Already heading for the door, and the answers to at least some of his questions, Jeremy jeered, "Nice to know where I stand."

"Isn't it?" Paige echoed cheerfully.

Jeremy said good-night and walked back across the pool area. Unbidden, the memory of Taylor stripping down to her skivvies popped into his consciousness. Resolutely, he pushed it back down. He continued on into the house, and entered Dani's office. The copy of Taylor's first novel was right where Paige had said.

He sat down in a comfortable armchair and studied the cover of the oversized trade paperback novel. There were two cartoon figures on the book—a studly guy on a sailboat, and a pretty girl with track shoes on, beneath the big block letter title. The Guy Who Sailed Away and the Girl Who Found Herself by Taylor O'Quinn.

One Texas newspaper had given it a four-star review and deemed it "Unforgettable." "Funny and real" said another. "Couldn't put it down!" declared a third reviewer.

Impressed, despite himself, Jeremy opened the book, and began to read.

TAYLOR AWAKENED to the blinding glare of sunlight and the sound of "Chasing Cars" by Snow Patrol. Groaning, she groped for the cell phone on the table beside the bed and flipped it open. The music ceased.

"Where are you?" the voice on the other end of the connection demanded.

Good question. Taylor blinked and keeping her cell phone pressed to her ear, pushed her way to a sitting position in the comfy queen-sized bed. She felt like a truck had run over her. Her entire body ached. And she was so stiff, it was hard to move.

Which was what she got, she concluded as she recognized the guest room in the Chamberlain ranch house, for driving halfway across the country in one day.

"Why weren't you at the wrap party for *Sail Away?*" Geraldine Meyerson demanded.

"How did you know about that?"

"It was on Mandy Stone's show on CEN last night," her editor at Sassy Woman Press replied with customary frankness. "Zoe and Zak said they were worried about you. Something about you crying as you were leaving the set?"

She'd been crying, all right. Taylor rubbed the sleep from her eyes. "Those were angry tears."

"I know Zak and Zoe have a rep for being difficult…"

"Difficult?" Taylor echoed. "Try insane!"

"It's all going to work out," Geraldine soothed.

"I don't see how," Taylor said miserably.

"It can't be as bad as you think," her editor insisted.

Taylor moaned. "You didn't see the dailies. You didn't have to participate in the rewrites."

"Just calm down and think about the hundred-thousand-copy reissue we're going to do. Those copies are going to fly off the shelf. And so are the copies of your second novel. How is your proposal for a third book coming?"

Taylor made a face. "I haven't had much time to work on it."

"The quicker you can get it in, the faster we'll be able to go to contract, get it written and get it to press, too. Meanwhile, it's imperative we have your first two books available to readers when the movie does come out."

"So you've said."

"Taylor, don't bail on me. I've stuck my neck out for you."

Taylor pulled herself together. "I'll get the new book proposal done as fast as I can."

"And don't skip any more movie or Zak and Zoe-related events that generate publicity," Geraldine ordered in her usual take-charge manner. "Sassy Woman Press, and your novels, need the attention."

JEREMY'S LAST PATIENT of the day was Krista Sue Wright. On the surface, the pretty twenty-two-year-old woman had everything going for her. A teaching job at the middle school in Laramie, an engagement to the new owner of the Laramie newspaper, a great family, lots of friends. However, the number of times she had been in his office since she had graduated from college the previous month indicated something was awry.

"I don't think it's broken." Krista Sue held up her swollen pinkie finger on her left hand. "But it hurts like the devil."

"It sure looks like it does," Jeremy sympathized, noting she'd had to take off the three-carat diamond engagement ring she had been sporting, and move it to her right ring finger instead. "How'd you do it?"

"It was silly, really. I caught it in the bathroom cabinet, between the hinge and the frame."

Jeremy examined her hand. "You're right—it's not broken. But it is sprained."

Krista Sue's face turned a blotchy pink and white. Her

lower lip trembled. "I don't know how I'm going to explain this to Brian. We were supposed to check out sites for the wedding reception this afternoon."

Jeremy put a splint on her finger. "When's the wedding?"

"July 24th."

"That doesn't give you much time."

"I know. But we really want to get married before I start teaching school in August and we're not fussy about the details. We just want our friends and family to be there."

Then why the big deal about missing the excursion this afternoon? Jeremy wondered. He got a couple of sample packs of ibuprofen and an instant ice pack out of the cupboard. "I think you can still keep that appointment. Just keep the cold on your sprain, twenty minutes on, twenty minutes off. And take the ibuprofen three times a day until the swelling and pain subsides. You'll be good as new in no time."

"Thanks, Dr. Carrigan."

"You're welcome." Jeremy paused. "Is everything else okay?"

Krista Sue looked at him, perplexed. "Why wouldn't it be?"

That was just it. He didn't know.

"How are the stomachaches you were having?" Jeremy asked casually.

"They subsided as soon as I stopped drinking so much caffeine. I don't even need the calcium carbonate tablets anymore."

Jeremy consulted the chart. "And the dermatitis on your elbows?"

"Gone, too, thanks to the skin lotion I've started using every day."

"And the migraines?"

"I only had the one. And it went away almost the moment I lay down in a dark room and closed my eyes. I think it was just…well, it's not easy living at home again with my folks, while I wait for the wedding to take place, after being on my own at college for four years."

"They pulling rank on you?" Jeremy teased.

Krista Sue rolled her eyes, her exasperation with her family evident. "Let's just say I haven't had to account for my whereabouts so much since I was sixteen! Anyway, thanks, doc, I won't keep you. I imagine Brian is waiting for me, over at the paper. I don't want to be late. He gets so grumpy when I keep him waiting."

Jeremy gave her a hand down from the examining table. "You'd tell me if there were anything else going on, wouldn't you?"

"Of course, but, there's not." Krista Sue rushed past him, gaze averted She used her uninjured hand to open the door, rushed out into the hallway, then stopped suddenly. She clapped a hand to her chest and announced excitedly, "Oh my gosh, I think I'm going to faint!"

TAYLOR HAD SEEN this kind of reaction plenty of times in the last two months—to Zoe and Zak, and various other celebrities in L.A. Never herself.

"You're Taylor O'Quinn!" The young woman dropped the ice pack she was holding and enthusiastically pumped Taylor's hand. "I'm Krista Sue Wright. You wrote that book! I loved it! Although I have to tell you, I had to go to so much trouble to find a copy. The only place I could find it was online."

Not surprising, Taylor thought, as Krista Sue finally let go of her hand. Meanwhile Jeremy bent to chivalrously retrieve her ice pack.

"I'm a new writer, so I got a very small print-run from Sassy Woman Press with my debut novel," Taylor explained, aware Jeremy was still standing there, watching her, a peculiar expression on his face. It was almost as if he were seeing her in a new light. She couldn't help but feel good about that. For reasons that weren't exactly clear, she had always wanted his respect.

Telling herself that it did not matter what Jeremy Carrigan— or anyone else—thought about her, Taylor turned her attention back to her enthusiastic fan.

Krista Sue looked starstruck. "The moment I read the review in *Dallas Women* magazine, I knew I had to get my hands on a copy. And I have to tell you—I was not disappointed. Your heroine was so funny and feisty and brave!"

"Thank you."

"And Rafael! Tell me you modeled him after a real guy!"

Taylor avoided the heat of Jeremy's gaze. "It's a work of fiction."

"But you must have known someone like him to be able to write such steamy…er…ahh." Krista Sue blushed fiercely, turning back to Jeremy as if suddenly realizing her family doctor was standing there, too, taking this all in.

The door to the reception area opened. A handsome young man, who looked to be in his mid to late twenties, walked in. He made a beeline for Krista Sue. "Are you okay?" He started to hug her, then noticed the ice pack she had pressed to her wrapped left hand. "Your mom said you hurt yourself reorganizing the bathroom shelves?"

"It's a long story." Krista Sue waved off the concern. "It was just a stupid household accident. And it's not important. What is important is…look who is here! It's the author of that book I love—the one that's being turned into a movie starring Zoe and Zak Townsend!"

He straightened. "You're right—it is." Pleasure lit his face. "I'm Brian Hilliard. I just purchased the Laramie newspaper. We'd love to do an in-depth interview with you."

"Well, I—" Taylor knew she had a duty to promote her book,

whenever possible. She owed her publisher that much. But she had come here to disappear, not step back into the limelight.

Brian Hilliard handed Taylor his business card with all his numbers.

"I'll need to check my calendar."

"Whatever works for you." Brian smiled. "Just let me know." He took Krista Sue by the elbow, intending to guide her to the checkout desk, where the receptionist was waiting to complete the necessary insurance paperwork.

Krista Sue turned back to Taylor. "I'm dying to know. The hero in your story was so sexy. Is he based on anyone you know? Or is he strictly a fantasy man?"

From the way Taylor flushed, Jeremy noted, you'd think it was some big mystery. When it wasn't. Everyone who knew Taylor personally, had long ago concluded the hero was a thinly disguised portrait of her ex-lover, Baywatch Bart.

Taylor ignored the taunting look Jeremy was giving her and met Krista Sue's curious gaze. "I get asked that a lot," Taylor admitted frankly.

"I'll bet," Krista Sue said. "It seemed so…real."

"But that romance began and ended in my imagination," Taylor concluded with a straightforward smile.

Which didn't quite answer the question, Jeremy thought. Although the retort seemed to satisfy Krista Sue.

"Did you need an appointment?" Ginny, the receptionist, asked Taylor, after Krista Sue Wright and her fiancé left.

"No. I'm just here to talk to Jeremy a minute," Taylor replied.

Would wonders never cease, Jeremy thought. Given the way Taylor had stomped off to bed the evening before, he'd figured it would be a long time before she ever gave him the time of day again. On the other hand, they were sharing space, albeit temporarily, at the Chamberlain ranch. Maybe she'd come to apologize to him for being so prickly. If so, that was something he wanted to hear.

"This way." He led Taylor into his private office and gestured for her to take a seat.

"I won't take but a minute of your time," she started, looking less than thrilled to be there.

"Take all the time you want." Jeremy took off his white lab coat, unbuttoned the first button on his dress shirt, and loosened his tie. Hoping to delay her at least long enough for them to call a truce, he sat, facing her. "I'm done for the day. The only thing I have ahead of me is a couple of hours' work on my ranch house."

She avoided his eyes, looking at everything in the office except him. "Paige asked me to be part of the celebrity auction the hospital is having to raise funds for the new wing. I know it won't be held until next September, but she said you are in charge of gathering the items to be sold, and I should talk to you about what I might donate."

Jeremy gripped the desk on either side of him and rocked forward slightly. He let his gaze drift over the elegant contours of her face. Aware all over again how much he had missed having her in his life, he said softly, "You could have talked to me about this back at the ranch."

She directed her attention to him once again. Her defenses were up. Oddly enough, that gave them something in common. He didn't know how he felt about her, either. Except that he wanted this tension between them to end…

"I was in town, doing errands," Taylor explained, looking flustered.

"Is that the only reason you came by my office?"

"Isn't it obvious?" She straightened. "I wanted to stare at your diplomas with envy."

Annoying her this way was starting to be fun. "No need to be sarcastic."

The lift of her brows said it all. "Sorry. The nosiness of others brings it out in me."

Jeremy chuckled. "Is this the way it's going to be?"

"What?" With an indignant sniff, she shot up out of her chair.

He caught her hand, tugged her toward him. "Us sparring back and forth continuously until you leave?"

She pushed him away, one hand flat against his chest. "I don't mind."

He let her go, reluctantly. "I do."

"Jeremy—"

It was all he could do not to take her in his arms. Aware how well that would go over, he contented himself with speaking what was on his mind. "I'd like us to be friends again."

Surveying him with exaggerated politeness, she crossed her arms in front of her. "Really?"

"Really."

"I don't see how that's possible, given the fact that you still—even after all this time—think I should have ignored my writing aspirations and gone into medicine."

Was that still true? Twelve hours ago, it had been. But now…

Jeremy thought about the chapter he had read the night before, Krista Sue Wright's reaction to Taylor's work, and the fact Taylor's very first novel was being turned into a movie. He stood slowly. "I was wrong, okay?" he said, surprised to find how good it felt to let go of the opinion that had torn them apart and kept them estranged for years. He had missed her. So much.

Figuring since he was responsible—at least in part—for driving her away, he should be part of the effort to bring her back, he continued, "It doesn't matter how good a doctor you would have been. You are obviously doing what you are meant to do."

Chapter Three

Zoe's Secret Anguish

Is the marriage of the music industry's hottest couple over? All of Hollywood seems to think so. Zoe Townsend hit the roof when she found Zak's lipstick and perfume-stained shirt on their hotel suite floor. Seems the color—and the fragrance—weren't hers....

June 3 edition,
International Inquisitor magazine

Before Taylor could respond to Jeremy's incredulous admission, his secretary buzzed in on his intercom. She wanted to discuss the next day's appointments prior to leaving for the evening.

Jeremy excused himself and left the office for a few minutes. When he returned, he gave Taylor a quizzical look. "What's wrong?"

Taylor's mouth dropped open. She looked like she didn't know whether to slug him or hug him. "Are you kidding me? How do you expect me to react to that bombshell you just dropped?"

Jeremy shook his head and continued in the same serious tone, "I'm the first to admit it when I am wrong. I was wrong."

She snorted indignantly. "After seven years of being a stubborn donkey's rear end, you change your mind," she snapped her fingers, "just like that."

Now, it was easy to come to that conclusion. Back then… how was he to know she was such a talented writer? Seven years ago, the only thing he had ever seen her put her energy toward was medical school. From the time she had entered college until the day she dropped out, Taylor had been exclusively focused on becoming a doctor. Just like him. He'd figured her abrupt decision to quit had been a combined reaction to stress, physical exhaustion, and fear. The thing was, they'd all felt that way during their grueling introduction to professional school, all wondered at some point at the start of their careers if they really had what it took to succeed in that field. For nearly all of them those feelings of indecision and insecurity had passed. He had assumed—for Taylor—that would be the case, too. Because he was her friend, he had tried to keep her from making a mistake that would destroy her long-held dream and haunt her the rest of her life.

Instead, from the looks of her—and the track record she had created as a writer—her actions had freed her.

Aware she was still waiting for the explanation behind his abrupt change of heart, he shrugged. "In those days, I hadn't read anything you'd written."

She edged closer. Her smile remained in place but he thought he saw it tighten a notch or two. "And now you have?"

Jeremy bit down on a curse. What was it about Taylor that always had him revealing too much? "I might have browsed a chapter of your book," he allowed.

She went very still. "And?"

"I'm as curious as Krista Sue Wright about the hero of your romance novel."

She frowned. "It's chick lit."

The contempt behind her reproach rankled, but he kept his irritation in check. "I stand corrected." He paused. "But you're dodging the question."

She flashed him a condescending smile. "Which is…?"

"In Chapter One your heroine is really drawn to the hero in a physical sense," he said.

"So?"

So everything about Taylor, from the silky fall of hair over her shoulders, to the clothes she wore, indicated she was a very sensual woman. He let his gaze rove the green cotton V-neck top that cut in slightly around the arms, leaving her shapely arms and shoulders bare. Her summer print skirt gloved her waist and hips in the same smooth, loving manner before ending just above her knees. Her legs were tan and bare, her delicate feet encased in sandals that looked as comfortable for walking as they were sexy. "So the hero in the book had a lot in common with that guy you were living with, back in Virginia," he said.

She glided past, in a drift of orange blossom perfume. "How would you know? You never met my ex."

Nor would he have wanted to. "Paige framed those pictures of you and Baywatch Bart. She's got them in the living room at her house. I couldn't help but notice them."

She turned slowly. "You sound…jealous."

Was he? "More like surprised," he corrected, in the lazy tone he used to push people away when they got too close. He met her probing gaze. "I never thought you'd go for the suntanned, superbuff, got-to-live-free dudes who have nothing more to do than spend their trust funds."

Taylor's eyes took on a turbulent sheen. "Bart didn't have

any family money. He was disinherited when he dropped out of law school. A lot of his friends, including his fiancée, wanted nothing further to do with him, too."

"Not unlike the hero in your novel," Jeremy noted.

"And me." She paused to examine the bronze statue one of his patients had brought him as a thank you. "My parents and two brothers pretty much stopped talking to me."

His heart went out to her. Being at odds with family sucked. "How is it now?" he asked her gently, dropping into doctor mode without meaning to.

She relaxed slightly. "Better, since my dad's heart attack last year. His illness really brought the family together. And it helped that I had a movie deal they could brag about to all their friends."

"So why don't you seem happier?" He went back to sitting on the edge of his desk. "Is it because you and Bart split up, and you're still pining after him?"

She moved behind his desk and dropped into the leather chair. She swiveled back and forth, testing the chair's ease. "Like the heroine in my novel, I don't need a man to make me happy."

"Does that mean you don't want one ever again?"

"No." She ran her finger along the edge of his desk. "It just means finding Mr. Right isn't all that high on my priority list."

When did her lips get so soft and so feminine? With effort, he returned his gaze to hers. "Then how come you stayed with Bart for so long?"

She challenged him with a knowing smirk. "Since you think my novel is really a roman à clef of my life with Bart, why don't you just read the rest of it and find out?"

"Because," he mocked her, "obviously, from the way you just said that, the book isn't about Bart."

She leaned forward, propping her elbow on his desk and resting her chin on her hand. "Bravo! You *finally* got it."

"Although…" He leaned closer, too. "Aren't all writers supposed to write what they know?"

She muttered a slew of words that indicated she hadn't just dated a sailor, she had learned to talk like one, too. "For the last time," she stood, slapping her palms on the surface of his desk, "*The Guy Who Sailed Away and the Girl Who Found Herself* is a work of fiction." She leaned forward until they were nose to nose. "F-I-C-T-I-O-N!"

Damn, but she looked pretty with all that agitated color brightening up her face, he noted. With effort, he remained where he was and resisted the temptation to touch her. Casually, he asked, "Why are you getting so defensive?"

Still glowering, she refused to answer.

Okay, maybe he should have read more of the book than the first chapter.

It wasn't that it hadn't been good. Her writing style was riveting—maybe because it sounded so much like the way Taylor spoke and acted herself. He had stopped because he didn't like the idea of Taylor with another guy, even in her imagination, which was just plain weird since he and Taylor had never dated. Yet here he was, reacting to her like he was romantically interested in her.

"Can we please just get on with this auction stuff?" Taylor said impatiently. "Paige said there is some paperwork I have to fill out if I want to participate."

Jeremy reached past her and opened his desk drawer. He retrieved the file that was on top and took out a handout for participants.

Their fingers brushed as she took it from him.

Ignoring the jolt of attraction, he said, "Just fill these out. It's pretty self-explanatory."

She nodded. "What kind of things are you looking for people to donate?"

"Whatever you think you can spare that will bring the most money. For instance, Dani Chamberlain is auctioning two tickets to a special screening of the biggest blockbuster movie of the summer, that generally only film critics and reviewers like herself get to attend. Beau Chamberlain is auctioning ten one-day visits to the soundstage of the movie he has in production. That will happen when he finishes all his location work up in Montana and returns to Laramie, in late July. His donation should bring in a boatload of money. My aunt Jenna is auctioning off one of her couture bridal gowns." Jeremy paused. "Do you have any memorabilia from your upcoming movie that you'd be willing to part with? Those items usually go for pretty big bucks."

"I didn't take anything from the set, when we finished filming."

"Not even a chair with your name on it or a copy of the script?"

Her eyes clouded over. "I didn't get a director's chair."

"What about an extra copy of the script?" he pressed.

"No." Her shoulders took on a defeated slump. "It would have been such a mess anyway…"

"Why?"

Taylor exhaled. "There were a lot of rewrites."

"That's pretty normal, isn't it?"

She chewed on her lower lip. "Not to the extent it happened on *Sail Away*."

Judging from her expression, her time in Hollywood had not been pleasant. "Why so many?"

She stood and retrieved her purse. "Zak and Zoe were in competition for screen time, number of lines, likeability of their character, you name it. Neither was happy unless he or she felt they held the advantage."

Was that what she was running from? Or was there something more? "That must have been hard to be around."

Her expression became inscrutable once again. She looped her shoulder bag over her arm and waved off his concern. "It's over now."

Was it? Something about the way she was acting said it wasn't. "So I guess there's no chance you could get Zoe and Zak to participate in the auction?"

Her expression went from sober to droll in no time flat. "Honestly, Jeremy, I wouldn't even ask."

TAYLOR LEFT Jeremy's office with the promise she would donate something to the auction, but no idea what that would be. She was nearly to her car when Jeremy jogged up behind her. "Got plans for this evening?"

"No." Wondering what he was up to now, she looked at him suspiciously. "Why?"

He grinned. "Ever torn down a wall?"

She looked at him quizzically. "Also…no."

Undeterred, he walked beside her as she made her way to the driver side. "Want to try it? You can paint my face on the drywall first. Might help you work off some of that aggression."

"When and where?" she asked.

"My ranch—as soon as we can get there. You want to follow me?"

Curious to see the land he'd purchased, she nodded. "Sure."

The drive out to Lake Laramie took twenty minutes. It was another ten to the entrance to Lago Vista Ranch. On her own, Taylor probably never would have found it. That's because the sign across the top of the welcoming wooden archway had been knocked off some time ago and lay splintered and broken in the waist-high weeds. And that was just the beginning of the air of neglect.

The gravel lane leading onto the property was choked on both sides with mesquite, cedar and sage. Closer to the lake, there were deep thickets of blackberry bushes, glistening with ripening fruit, just begging to be picked. Midway onto the private property, the lane diverged in two directions. Jeremy took the one to the right. As they bumped along the path, one vehicle after another, the ground sloped downward. Finally, they topped a rise and a steep decline. The sprawling lake was in view. Under the deep blue Texas sky, the lake was a shimmering aqua blue.

At the lake end of the lane was a weathered dock. Taylor parked and got out to soak up the view.

Part of the lake was open to the public and set aside for camping, hiking and other recreational activities. The rest of the property fronting the water—like Lago Vista Ranch— was privately owned. From where they stood, she could see vacation homes dotting the shore. The occasional marina. Private boat slips. A popular restaurant overlooking the lake. Out on the water, there were sailboats and cruisers. Everything you would expect on a perfect summer evening.

"I can see why you bought the ranch," Taylor murmured appreciatively. "The view alone…"

"I come here and sit some evenings to decompress."

Taylor liked to do the same thing when she was writing. "There's something so soothing about the water," she murmured. In fact, the proximity to Virginia Beach was why she had settled in the Chesapeake area of Virginia.

His smile was slow and sexy. "Want to see the rest of the property?"

"Sure."

They backed up their vehicles, and turned around carefully.

Taylor led the way back to the fork in the lane, and still in the lead, followed the path they had yet to take.

Once again, the property had a deep aura of neglect, or maybe it was just wilderness. There was barbed wire along the edges, along with the occasional weathered No Trespassing sign, but no effort had been made to cultivate the property into the well-manicured ranchland prevalent in Laramie County.

Even if someone came in and took down the underbrush, thinned out some of the trees, and mowed the high grass in the meadows, it wouldn't stay that way, Taylor noted.

Jeremy must have one hundred acres here, she guessed, as they came upon another rise. And there, in the middle of a small clearing, was one of the oddest dwellings she had ever seen.

The central part of the one-story ranch house was rectangular in shape and built of white stone. It had double windows on either side of the massive oak door, and a wide front porch shaded by a steep tin roof. Toward the back, there were two narrow wings, jutting out at ninety-degree angles from the main part of the house. These were made of stucco. One was painted bright turquoise, the other bright coral.

"Go ahead." Jeremy held the door as she got out of the driver side of her Jeep. He exhaled in resignation, appearing to brace himself. "There's nothing you can say I haven't heard before."

Taylor walked around the weed choked front lawn. It looked like an acre had been cleared around the domicile. Beyond that was the same overgrown tangle of scrub, trees and weeds she had encountered on the rest of the property.

"It's…interesting."

Jeremy fell into step beside her. "It's bizarre."

She walked around toward the back. As she got closer, she noted the stucco had been applied over what looked like pale orange brick. Patches of it shone through, around the edges. "I'd love to hear the story behind this." She indicated the home.

Jeremy stuffed his hands in the pockets of his trousers. Taking her hand, he drew her out of the heat and into the shade. "The original owner built the four rooms in the center. He primarily used the place as a fishing and hunting retreat.

It's pretty rustic. He wasn't much on upkeep and he sold it to a couple who dabbled in amateur architecture. The husband loved the South Beach area of Florida. The wife adored historic Charleston, South Carolina. They wanted to expand the house. They couldn't agree how. So they compromised by building his-and-her wings in the stucco-over-brick-style of historic Charleston and painted them the vivid tropical colors of South Beach."

"Wow."

He let go of her hand as casually as he had clasped it. "The previous owners ended up getting divorced, and the property had to be sold as part of the settlement. Naturally, given the air of neglect there weren't many prospective buyers even willing to consider taking on such a big project. I came along," he announced proudly, "and got it for a song."

Taylor stepped onto the V-shaped patio located between the two wings. There was no doubt the property could be turned into something, but it would take one hell of a lot of work. "How long have you had it?" she asked.

"Two years."

She noted the pile of construction debris located next to the back door. It certainly appeared to be a work-in-progress. "And you've never lived here?"

"Once I show you the inside, you'll understand why." Jeremy unlocked the patio doors. The air inside was stifling. It felt like the heat of an oven rushing out at them. Inside the main room, the floor had been stripped down to the cement slab. There was no kitchen to speak of, just a cooler where a refrigerator should have been and a freestanding metal sink more suited to a laundry room, with an old-fashioned spigot. The remaining drywall had big gouges in it.

"You tore out all the cabinets?"

"They were rainbow-painted aluminum," he explained.

"Oh."

"The refrigerator had been shut off, still filled with food, in the summer heat. There was so much mold and bacteria in it, it had to go, too. Not that it would have been worth much—it was in pretty bad shape. There's no central heat or air."

"Then…?" she asked.

"The fireplace is it, when it comes to heat."

Taylor blinked. "For the whole house?"

"Wings and all, yep."

He led her toward the front of the house. "Initially, these two rooms were bedrooms, the Realtor said." Jeremy indicated the two closed-off rooms on either side of the front door. "I think they should be formal rooms, living and dining, so I plan to take out the center part of each wall here to open them up."

Taylor got the picture. "Which is where the sledgehammers come in."

"Right."

She looked around. "There's no guest bathroom, I gather?"

"No. The original owner went with the outhouse for that. I tore that down and put in a port-a-potty."

Taylor took a moment to consider that as she walked back toward the main living area. Although still stifling-hot, the fresh air flowing in from outside was cooling the space slightly. "How did they bathe, if they didn't have a bathroom?"

"Lake?" Jeremy guessed. "I don't know. Fortunately, the second owners—the couple who ended up getting divorced—had a full bath put in each wing."

"So you have plumbing out here?"

"I will—when I get a new septic tank put in."

Taylor nodded, thinking, "No wonder you got it for a steal."

"Let me show you the rest." Jeremy led the way into one wing. It was a large bedroom, painted a hideous color of purple, with matching carpet and walls. The theme continued into the adjacent bath. Taylor couldn't help but stare. "I didn't know they made counters and bathtubs that color."

"Apparently you can paint them. Or get them recovered. I haven't figured out what I'm going to do. I'd like to tear it all out and put in marble. Or maybe ceramic tile. I'm not sure."

They ventured across to the opposite wing. It was done all in hot pink. Taylor was so busy looking around, she ran into him. He reached out a hand to steady her.

"I keep saying this," she shook her head, "but wow."

"I know." He grimaced.

Taylor focused on the bright side. "Both bedrooms have a good layout. They're spacious. They each have a bath. Big windows. Plenty of light."

"So you think it has potential?" Jeremy asked cautiously.

Taylor walked back out into the main room. "Absolutely, I do. The only thing I don't understand is why you aren't living here right now."

JEREMY STARED at Taylor, stunned. "Well that's the first time anyone's ever expressed any kind of enthusiasm for this place."

A comfortable silence settled between them. "What do they usually say?" she asked.

He winced, recalling. "Everything from bulldoze the house and start over, to sell and find something habitable."

She eyed him considering from beneath her thick black lashes. "They don't get you want to turn this property around yourself?"

If only she'd been here all along…he could have used her innate understanding. "Not just turn it around," he confided. "Make it into my dream home."

Taylor shot him a quick, reproving glance. "Well, you're never going to get there if you keep going at the rate you've been! You're going to have to *live* here."

She wasn't kidding. "Without working plumbing or central air?"

Her frown softened and faded behind a slow smile. "I'm guessing you have the means to take care of both pretty promptly if you want to. I saw the electric wires running onto the ranch, so I know it wouldn't be that big a deal to get the power going. I'm serious, Jeremy. If you want to make this dream come true, you're going to have to work on it every single day, not just when the mood strikes."

"Not so easy. I'm a doctor with a full medical practice."

She shrugged. "Then hire it done, bit by bit."

He dug in stubbornly. "I want to do it myself."

She scoffed. "Sounds like procrastination to me."

Procrastination was exactly what it was. The thing was, the way he was taking his time wasn't bothering *him* near as much as it was everyone else in his life. His hands still thrust in the pockets of his trousers, he strode closer. "Suppose I'm content to bide my time? What then?"

She stepped nearer and taunted softly, "Then I would think you are afraid."

Like hell he was. He met her challenge. "Of what?"

Complacency echoed in her low tone. "Failure."

He shook his head at her. "I'm not a failure."

"Maybe not as a physician," she allowed, coming closer yet. She tipped her head back to better see into his face. She tapped a teasing finger against the center of his chest. "I can't say the same about your nesting skills."

He caught her hand before she could steal it away again, held it there. "Nesting is for women."

He felt her resistance, even though she made no move to pull away. "Everyone needs a home, Jeremy."

He mocked her. "Says the person without a place to go right now."

This time, she did withdraw her hand from his easy grip. "I don't have a permanent residence because I gave up the house I was renting in Virginia, to move to Los Angeles. I was thinking I might like to buy a place there, but I changed my mind after living there."

Okay, maybe that was half the story.... "Too expensive?" he guessed.

"Too superficial. At least the part of Los Angeles I was in."

He saw the vulnerability in her expression he knew she wanted to hide, and wished he had some way to protect her, without overstepping his bounds. "Was that the only reason you left in a hurry?"

She lifted the hair from the back of her neck and stepped outside. "Back to that again."

He joined her on the patio, glad the heat of the sun was finally starting to lessen. He watched her take an elastic band from her wrist and use it to secure her glossy mane in a ponytail high on the back of her head. "I still think you're running from something," he said.

Taylor made a face at him. "Says the person who is afraid to put in a working septic system and central AC."

"Okay," Jeremy countered, before he could think. "I'll make a deal with you. I'll get that done. I'll get this place move-in-ready. *If* you will agree to go out with me."

TAYLOR FELT LIKE ONE of those bottom-weighted plastic clowns that took a punch and swung right back up. "Go out with you?" she echoed, before she could stop herself.

"As in date me. And don't look so surprised. You can't tell me you haven't felt some serious vibes between us, too."

Okay, so she had. But that did not mean she had to abandon all common sense and behave recklessly. The practical side of her was saying she was not signing up to get her heart crushed by him again. It had been bad enough, feeling like they had disappointed each other when they had just been pals.

Taylor thought about how hard she had worked to forge a satisfying, independent life for herself since she and Bart had split up. With effort, she pulled herself together, and shifted the attention back to him. "What I think is that the Texas heat is getting to you."

He kept his eyes on her face. "What's the harm in going out?"

The heat of a blush warmed her cheeks. She walked back into the house. "I would say we'd ruin our friendship but we pretty much already did that."

He followed her with a shrug. "So we have nothing to lose."

"Except our dignity?" She sauntered over to examine the aging metal sink. "Seriously, Jeremy, you and I are not the least bit suited for each other."

Affection softening his face, he closed in on her slowly. "Maybe we are. Maybe the reason neither of us has gotten married is that we've been dating people who are too much like ourselves. Maybe we should go for our polar opposite style instead."

A thrill sifted through her. "We're opposite all right."

"You're emotion-driven and artistic. I'm practical and analytical."

She leaned in for a closer look. "As well as out of your mind."

His quiet laughter filled the space between them. "You're just afraid you might like it."

She swallowed and worked on steadying her knees. "Us going out? I wouldn't hold my breath, if I were you."

He took a coin out of his pocket. "Want to flip for it?"

"No," she said through a sigh.

"Do rock-paper-scissors?" His palm slid to her elbow then dropped to his side.

"Definitely not!"

He towered over her and made her feel petite. "Then how about a test run?"

Delicate tingles rippled through her. Her gaze stared into his. "What do you mean by that?"

"One kiss."

Her breath caught in her throat, reminding her just how long she'd been without a man in her life, just how long she had wanted a pursuit like this. Pretending she had no urge to explore anything with him, she shook her head in silent reproof. "Now I know you're nuts!"

He wrapped his arms around her and brought her flush against him. Shifting her hair aside, he kissed his way down her throat. "If you don't feel anything," he promised against her nape, "I'll take no for an answer."

Desire caught fire inside her. "What if you don't feel anything?"

He leaned his forehead against hers. He ran his thumb along the line of her jaw. "I'm already feeling something."

"Jeremy—"

"Taylor."

His mouth closed on hers before she could murmur another word. He kissed her long and hard and she kissed him back just as passionately, savoring the scent of his skin and the strength of his arms. The feel of his tall, muscular form pressed against her sent sensations rippling through her body. Suddenly, the years they'd been apart fell away, and they were back in time, to when they hadn't known yet how to stay away from each other. Taylor was determined not to let him get to her, not to let him win, but already the battle seemed lost.

She had waited a lifetime to be kissed like this. But she had never in her wildest dreams imagined that it would be with him.

Chapter Four

Caught in the Act!

As the above photo attests, the scandal surrounding Zak Townsend is not all in wife, Zoe's, mind. The rocker/reality TV star/film actor has been involved in a dalliance with an ebony-haired beauty. Although to date, her identity remains a mystery…

Scandal! magazine

"I can't believe you're actually going on a date with Jeremy," Paige said, in the Chamberlain ranch house, hours later.

If it hadn't been for that kiss, and her reaction to it…

Taylor pushed aside the evocative memory of the taste and feel of his mouth moving over hers. So she'd been momentarily weak…vulnerable. "I said I'd go when he got the septic tank and the heating and air-conditioning unit installed at Lago Vista Ranch. We both know that will never happen."

Paige sprinkled southwestern seasoning blend and olive oil on tilapia filets and slid them onto a sizzling hot grill pan. "It might."

Taylor put together a salad of field greens, toasted pine nuts and fresh orange slices. "Trust me. I've met tons of guys like Jeremy in the last seven years, and heard about dozens more. They're extremely successful in their profession, but the rest of their life is disorganized and unfocused. They *say* they want something like a ranch or a boat or a wife and family, but they never actually focus their energy and *do* anything to achieve it. Instead, they put all their efforts toward their work. And then wonder why they're not happy." She shook her head on an exhalation of breath.

"The same could be said about us." Paige dropped a pint of fresh yellow tomatoes in the food processor.

Mincing a shallot and a clove of garlic, Taylor said defensively, "I don't have any illusions about marriage."

Paige chopped two Serrano chilis, a couple tablespoons of cilantro and added them to the bowl. She squeezed in lime juice and added salt and pepper. "You don't want a husband?"

Taylor shrugged. She couldn't deny there were times, when she saw some of her happily married friends with babies, that she yearned for a more settled lifestyle. She also had friends who had married in haste or for all the wrong reasons and later paid the price. She was not going to get caught in that trap. "I refuse to settle."

Paige wiped her hands on a towel. "What does that mean?"

"I want to be head over heels in love," Taylor admitted.

Paige nodded, understanding.

Taylor put the lid on the food processor and pushed pulse until the salsa was of the desired consistency. "I also happen to be realistic enough to know the odds of my finding my own Mr. Right are not anywhere near as great as I'd like."

"Meaning what?" Paige gave her a shrewd glance and went back to flip the sizzling fish. "You either settle for less? Or live the rest of your life alone?"

Did it have to be that cut and dried? More than anything,

Taylor wished it would just happen for her—and for the rest of the single women out there—the same way it did in all the great books and movies. But what if she never found someone? What if all she had was the one tantalizing possibility that had haunted her for years now? Determined not to give herself away, Taylor said finally, "I'm not alone. I have friends like you."

"And Jeremy," Paige reminded. "*If* you two don't blow it again."

"My relationship with Jeremy is complicated."

Paige laughed. "I'll say."

"We always rub each other the wrong way."

Paige paused a moment, then smiled. "Maybe because you two 'get' each other in a way few people do."

It didn't always feel like that. Taylor paused. "If you're talking about the fact that we see each other's flaws—"

"And strengths." Paige tested the salsa and added more salt. "He really respects the success you have achieved as a writer."

So Jeremy had said to her earlier. Wondering how much— if anything—that changed things between them in the overall scheme of things, Taylor chided Paige. "When did you get so romantic?" In the past, like Taylor and Jeremy, Paige had concentrated on building a career for herself. Friends and family were next in the hierarchy. Relationships with the opposite sex had run a distant fourth.

"That's what comes of being the only child of a couple who remain madly in love with each other to this day. I want what my parents have. I won't settle for less, either."

"I'm glad we're in total agreement on that point!" Taylor beamed at Paige, feeling an even deeper kinship with her close friend.

Paige poured a glass of wine for both of them. She lifted her glass in a toast. "To strong, independent, like-minded women."

"Here, here," Taylor said. They clinked glasses.

Jeremy walked in. Fresh out of the shower, he had Taylor's cell phone in his hand. He looked really ticked off. "You've got to start answering this thing. Either that or shut off the ringer. It's been going off nonstop for the last twenty minutes. If I have to listen to that song one more time…"

"Sorry."

As Jeremy handed it over, the phone began to ring—again.

Taylor looked at the caller ID and swallowed an oath. "I'll take this outside," she said.

"TAYLOR, LUV, you've got to start answering your phone," Zak Townsend reprimanded.

Taylor tensed. She had hoped her days of having to deal with the egocentric celebrity and his equally demanding and self-absorbed wife were over. At least until the premiere of *Sail Away*. And despite pressure from her publisher, she hadn't yet decided if she would be attending that or not. "I'm on vacation."

"You *wish* you were on vacation. There's more work to be done."

Unease trickled through her. "In post-production, yes."

"We're not done filming."

"We had the wrap party."

"Which you blew off."

Taylor's jaw tightened. "You know why I didn't attend."

Zak scoffed. "You're being provincial."

The nightmare scenario descended full force, once again. "Call it whatever you want. I don't appreciate what you did."

"I didn't do anything. You came on to me!"

Taylor rubbed her temples. She felt a tension headache coming on. Which was no surprise. She always got them when her life was headed in the wrong direction. She worked to keep the shrill note of temper from her voice. Three months of dealing with these people and their production company was too much. "Nothing happened," she reminded him firmly. "Nothing is going to happen, Zak."

His voice dropped a seductive notch. "I think you're fooling yourself, denying your feelings this way."

Think anything you like, jerk. "If that's all…"

"It's not. The studio is unhappy with the dailies they have seen. They want more shooting—at least two or three days' worth. They want to know why the lead characters in *Sail Away* are behaving like they do."

So did Taylor, as it happened. The constant rewrites demanded by the stars of the production had turned her original script into a muddled, incomprehensible mess.

"So Zoe and I came up with a brilliant idea. We've decided to send our characters to the desert for the denouement of the film."

Taylor didn't know whether to laugh or cry. "You understand the film is titled *Sail Away*."

"Yes, well, we might have to change that." Zak paused, temporarily stymied. "Although I suppose it is possible we could find an oasis or a lake."

"Good luck with that. I'm done. Really."

"Read your contract with Always Famous Production Company. You're not done until we say you're done, Taylor. And you certainly won't be paid the rest of your advance until a satisfactory script is finished. You may not care about that money…"

Actually, Taylor did. She really…*really*…needed to get paid. If not for Paige's generosity, and that of her parents, she'd soon be sleeping in her Jeep Liberty. "Fine. But I'm not coming back to Hollywood. Just tell me what you need. I'll fax my pages in to you."

"That won't be necessary, luv. We're coming to you."

Dread spiraled through her. "How do you know where I am?"

"I called Geraldine Meyerson. She tells me Sassy Woman Press has arranged quite a nice print-run for the reissue of your first novel and we've agreed to work with her to make sure the sale of the book coincides closely with the release of the movie."

Great. Now her writing career really was going to be ruined.

"Although first we have to finish the movie, which is why we've arranged to do the last few days of reshooting at Beau Chamberlain's film studio in Texas."

"You're coming to Laramie?" He might as well just drive a stake in her heart.

"It'll be fun. Although I hear the hotel accommodations in town are rather…rustic."

The hotel rooms were fine. Clean, spacious, comfortable. They just didn't have things like personal saunas and racquetball courts.

"We'll be arriving sometime tomorrow. I'm not sure when. It depends on when Zoe wakes up. Although I imagine she'll want to avoid the paparazzi when the latest edition of *Scandal* hits the stands tomorrow morning."

"What's in that?" Taylor hated to ask.

Zak groaned. "A photo, luv, that never should have been taken."

A PHOTO OF WHAT? Taylor wondered, cutting the connection on her cell phone. Did she even want to know? She stood, shoulders slumped, staring off into the night.

A throat cleared behind her.

Taylor turned to find Jeremy standing there. "Paige wants you to know dinner is ready." Keys in hand, he headed past her, toward the drive.

Unable to understand the shift in his mood, which had

been darn good right up until the moment he headed for the shower, she said, "You're not staying?"

He kept right on walking. "Changed my mind."

His gruff tone hurt even more than his aloof attitude. "Jeremy—"

He turned, looked her right in the eye. His expression was impassive.

There was an underlying contempt to his regard that hadn't been there earlier. How much had he overheard of what she'd said just now? What conclusions had he jumped to? She moved closer. "Are you ticked off at me?"

He stared at her. "Should I be?" He ambled closer. "I mean, it's not like you and Paige would be sitting around, talking about what a loser I am."

So he'd heard their conversation about her not wanting to settle for Mr. Wrong. Taylor wanted to sink through the ground. "I think you misconstrued what we said."

Resentment glimmered in his dark brown eyes. "I don't think so." He turned and started walking away again. "And for the record, I always follow through on what I say I'm going to do."

His sarcasm stung. Worse was the knowledge she'd hurt him, verbalizing her low expectations. "Jeremy, please." Her heart racing, Taylor went after him, arms outstretched. "Stay and eat with us." *Let me make this right.*

"Nope."

"I'm sorry. Really."

He shrugged his broad shoulders. "Nothing to be sorry about." He got into his pickup truck without a backward glance and drove off.

"Who lit a fire under you?" Meg Carrigan asked half an hour later.

Jeremy looked at his mother, his patience wearing thin. "Are you going to help me or not?"

"Help who with what?" Luke strolled onto the screened-in back porch, a medical journal tucked under his arm.

"Jeremy wants the name of a heating and air-conditioning company," Meg explained, making room for Luke. "There are two in town. I told him they're both fine."

"They are." Luke sat down on the porch swing next to Meg and draped his arm along the back. "The question is, what are you planning to do?"

"Isn't it obvious?" Jeremy asked, irritated both his parents were acting so clueless when he was pretty certain they knew exactly why he was requesting a referral at long last.

Meg put a hand to the center of her chest. "Tell me you're not going to throw good money after bad."

Jeremy sat on the edge of a chaise, forearms resting on his thighs. "If you're asking if I'm inquiring because I want to fix up my ranch, the answer is yes."

Luke cleared his throat. "I have to agree with your mother, son. It's time you sold the property to someone who can actually clear the land and ranch it. Better to find yourself something a little less labor intensive."

Like what? Jeremy wondered. "There are no other ranches with lake views in commuting distance of Laramie."

"But there are plenty of other ranches," Meg countered. "Many with comfortable houses that are move-in ready. You could be living there, instead of going from place to place, like a gypsy."

His track record with domiciles wasn't that bad, and they knew it. "I stayed at Trevor and Rebecca's ranch house at Wind Creek for almost a year. In fact, I'd still be there if they hadn't decided to turn it into quarters for the full-time ranch hands they now employ."

"There's no question your sister and her husband were very generous to let you lease the house, when it was vacant.

It doesn't change the fact that you purchased a residence in which you can not live!" Luke admonished him.

"That's not going to be the case any longer," Jeremy maintained. "As soon as I get a new septic tank put in—and a heating and air conditioning unit hooked up—I'm moving in."

"Are you going to hire contractors to do the rest of the work for you?" Meg asked.

"No." Jeremy was getting really tired of people doubting him. "I'm doing it myself."

Luke's exasperation mounted. "You realize, of course, you will never get a woman interested in marrying you if you continue to live that way."

"Maybe that's the whole point." Meg measured the baby blanket she was knitting. "Maybe Jeremy wants to keep from making a commitment."

"If you're thinking of matchmaking for me, the way you did for Susie, and would have done for Rebecca and Amy had they not beat you to the punch and found their own mates, you can forget it," Jeremy warned.

"It might not be a bad idea," Meg protested. "There's a young real estate agent who just moved here. I met her the other day. She's about your age. Single. Very nice. Very personable and good-looking."

"I don't need you to introduce us." Jeremy stood, realizing too late that he should have gone to one of his siblings for a recommendation. They all lived on ranches. They all had water from wells and special environmentally-friendly septic systems to recycle the waste into water that could be used for irrigation. They would have known instantly whom he should call. But he hadn't prevailed on them because he hadn't wanted to get the "business" from them, about the property that they, too, considered little more than worthless. "I already have a date for later this week—with Taylor O'Quinn," Jeremy said, just to get them off his back.

"Taylor's back in town?" Meg looked delighted.

"For a few weeks," Jeremy admitted, wondering how he could have misread Taylor's response to their kiss so drastically. He'd thought she was beginning to have a thing for him, too.

Aware his mother was waiting for more information, he said, "Taylor's staying with Paige."

"I forgot to tell you," Luke looked at Meg. "I saw Taylor at the hospital today. She agreed to donate something for the celebrity auction that the hospital is holding in September."

Meg smiled. "I've always liked her. She is such a sweet girl. I remember when she used to come home from college with Paige."

Jeremy stood. "Yeah, well, don't go getting your hopes up, Mom," he warned. "It's just a date." One he was determined Taylor was going to follow through with—even if it went nowhere. "Before we know it, Taylor will probably be moving on again." But that didn't mean he couldn't enjoy being with her while she was here, see where their one-helluva-kiss led. To do otherwise would practically guarantee he would never get her out of his mind. One way or another he had to know... was there something between them?

TAYLOR KNEW it was one of those nights when sleep was not going to come easily. So she did what she always did under the circumstances; she made good use of her time. All the while, trying not to think about how long it was going to take for Jeremy to forgive her for her presumptiveness.

Whether her prediction came true about him never actually getting around to making his fixer-upper ranch livable was not the point. She hated being disrespected for what she had yet to accomplish, no matter how far-fetched the dream. She had no right doing it to anyone else.

So, while trying to figure out how to apologize to him in a way he would accept, she got out her laptop and surfed the Web. Window shopping a little at first, then doing her best to satisfy her curiosity and figure out…

"You miss Hollywood that much, hmm?" The low, familiar voice teased from behind her.

Jeremy. To her relief, he didn't sound piqued with her any longer. Nevertheless, this was not a good time! As coolly as possible, she tried to block his view of the screen on her laptop computer. Too late. Jeremy had seen what she had been reading, as well as what she was wearing—her usual bedtime attire of boxer shorts and a tank top.

Embarrassed to be caught looking like an escapee from a beauty salon, she fumbled for the belt on her thigh-length kimono, but not before he had noted exactly how much of her just-shaved legs were exposed and that she wasn't wearing a bra. Something lit in his eyes she would have preferred not to see.

"Caught in the act!" Jeremy read, tamping down an amused smile, while skimming over the initial info on the cheating celebrity spouse. "…dalliance with an ebony-haired beauty. Although to date the woman's identity remains a mystery…"

Jeremy did a double take, zeroing in on the photo, the hint of profile, the telltale gold shamrock necklace clearly visible in the open V of the mystery woman's blouse. He turned and stared at Taylor, the same way the two crew members who had walked onto the empty soundstage, where Zak had cornered her, had done. "You're fooling around with Zak Townsend?" Jeremy inquired, stunned.

"No, of course not!" Self-consciously, Taylor removed the cotton she had woven through her toes, to protect her just-polished toenails from smudging. Figuring this was what she got for leaving her bedroom door wide open, while having a spa night, she walked into the adjacent bath. "Lovely," she murmured to her reflection. Blue goop, covered all but her eyes and her lips. She wet a washcloth and began taking off the pore-refining facial mask.

Jeremy came into the bathroom and lounged in the doorway, as casually as he had during their med school days when he and Paige and Taylor—along with others—lived together in a big house. Jeremy folded his arms in front of him. "It sure looks like Zak Townsend's holding you in his arms and kissing your ear."

Taylor knew the photo made it look as if she had been enjoying the caress. That had not been the case. The gasp the photographer had captured on her face had been one of shock, not ecstasy. "I didn't know he was going to do that. And I certainly didn't know anyone with a camera was lurking in the shadows, waiting to send a photo of Zak hitting on me off to *Scandal* magazine." Although that hadn't been what the tabloid alleged. The tabloid had hinted Taylor *wanted* to get caught with Zak, so she could push Zoe out of the marriage and have Zak Townsend all to herself. Taylor rinsed her face and blotted with a soft, fluffy towel. "I loathe the man."

Jeremy picked up the washcloth. He dabbed a spot she had missed, just beneath her chin. "Was he the person who kept calling your cell phone this evening?" Finished, Jeremy tossed the cloth aside.

Taylor plucked her bottle of facial moisturizer from her toiletries bag and sighed. "Zak wanted to let me know that the studio is demanding they rewrite and reshoot key scenes of *Sail Away* for the next two or three days."

"So you're going back to Los Angeles?"

"Worse." Taylor turned back to the mirror and spread moisturizer over her cheeks. "They're all coming here to shoot at Chamberlain Studio and do some location work out in the desert west of here. At least that's the plan this evening. Who knows what it will be by tomorrow morning."

Jeremy braced a hip on the edge of the counter next to her. "Is that why you came here? Because you knew you were going to have to work?"

"No...I thought I was finished. I want to be finished." Taylor picked up her lip balm. "This is such a nightmare."

Jeremy seemed to think so, too. The difference was, he appeared ready to take action against her opponents. "Does Zoe know Zak is putting the moves on you?"

It wouldn't have mattered. Taylor shrugged and used the tip of her index finger to coat her lips. "Their marriage is a sham." She pressed her lips together to further set the conditioning agent. "Neither of them appear to be monogamous, at least from what I can glean."

Jeremy tore his glance from her lips, with effort. "They were always so lovey-dovey on their reality TV show. Kissing in public and stuff."

Taylor shrugged and snapped the lid on the container. "You followed that?"

"The teenage patients do. Sometimes I'll catch a little bit of it, during evening rounds. From what I gather, Zak and Zoe are the romantic ideal for the 14-18 age group."

"More like 12-16, but yeah, the two of them really know how to sell a product."

Jeremy's gaze narrowed. "If you know this, how did you ever put yourself in a position to be hit on by him?"

Taylor took the clip out of her hair. "Because he's the head of their production company, Always Famous. And he is my boss. Temporarily anyway."

Jeremy's jaw clenched. "That sounds like sexual harassment."

Taylor ran a brush through her hair. "It's more complicated than that. I sold their company the movie rights to my novel

and signed on to be the screenwriter. Zak and Zoe were so enthusiastic about my story that they assured me that they would
bring it to the big screen in a way that was true to my novel.
To ensure that was the case, they asked me to sign on as
screenwriter and story consultant. The pay wasn't Hollywood-
fabulous, but it was more than I got from Sassy Woman Press,
so I gave up my lease in Virginia and headed west. My moti-
vation being that if it worked out, I could get freelance work
as a script doctor or something, while I was developing a book
proposal and waiting to go to contract on my third novel."

"It didn't turn out that way."

"No." Taylor set her brush down with a sigh. "It was a
nightmare from day one. Zoe and Zak fought over everything. They've changed the story so many times, it's a friggin'
mess. Now, quite understandably I might add, the studio is
upset and demanding that they reshoot key scenes. Meanwhile, Zak and Zoe are on another tangent that is just going
to muddy the story line even more. And the tabloids are hint-
ing I am having an affair with Zak!"

Jeremy followed her back into the bedroom. "Can't you
just quit?"

Taylor sat on the upholstered bench at the foot of the bed. "Not
if I ever want to work again. Bottom line—I signed a contract.
I knew this could happen. Paige tried to tell me. She knew from
the industry gossip her folks are privy to that Zak and Zoe were
not trustworthy people. But I was so desperate to prove to
everyone that I hadn't blown my entire future by dropping out
of med school, that I was a writer of note, that I took the risk
against all common sense. Now I'm paying for it, big time."

AND JEREMY HAD THOUGHT *he* had problems. He sat down
on the bench beside her, took her hand in his. "What can I
do to help?"

"What kind of *help* are you referring to?" she asked.

He felt her pulse quicken beneath his fingertips. "Do you want me to pose as your lover?" What had started out as an altruistic proposition, quickly turned into something else. The desire to hold her in his arms and kiss her again assailed him.

Her expression turned droll. "In whose lifetime?"

He kept his eyes locked with hers. "The one thing that sends a guy in another direction is the realization the woman he has his eye on is already taken. It's a territory thing, Taylor." He stood and let his hands rest lightly on her shoulders. "Guys don't intrude on another guy's turf."

Once again, she slipped free of his touch. "Maybe honorable guys don't." She sighed and ran her hands through her silky black hair. "Zak would probably only see your interest in me as competition and be emboldened."

Jeremy couldn't help but note how pretty she looked, with her fresh, glowing skin, bright eyes and bare, soft lips. "So what are you going to do?"

She shrugged off the question. "Make sure I am not alone with him ever again."

He wished he could kiss her. "Is that possible?"

"It's got to be." She raked her teeth across the plumpness of her lower lip. "Otherwise…"

"He'll be hitting on you again," Jeremy guessed.

Her eyes darkened. She pointed toward the image still on her computer screen. "Hopefully, that tabloid photo will send him in another direction. Zak and Zoe don't want their infidelities made public. It would erode their audience. If there is one thing those two care about, it's staying in the limelight."

Jeremy smirked. "Hence the name of their production company. Always Famous."

"Not too subtle, are they?" They exchanged cynical smiles. "You're up awfully late," Taylor noted, after a moment.

It was Jeremy's turn to shrug. "I had to see a man about an eco-friendly septic tank system."

"You're kidding."

As much as he was loath to admit it, Taylor's comments to Paige tonight had given him a much-needed kick in the pants. "Nope. It'll be in and running by the end of the week." He came nearer, drinking in the enticing citrus scent of her shampoo. He tucked a hand beneath her chin, tilted her face up to his. "And you know what that means, don't you?"

Her speculative expression said she knew, all too well. "Time to focus on the installation of the heating and air-conditioning system?" She matched his silky-soft taunt to a T.

He dropped his hand, stepped back, and gave her one last, lingering look. "Time to get ready for that date you owe me."

Chapter Five

Mystery Woman Revealed!

The black-haired beauty caught in a clinch with Zak Townsend has been identified by those in the know as novelist-turned-screenwriter, Taylor O'Quinn. Caught making out behind the scenes of *Sail Away*, the hot-blooded mistress fled to her native state of Texas, where she promptly made time with yet another lover…as the following photos attest…

The Celebrity Dish Web site
update, June 5

"If you want to interview me for this week's edition of the Laramie newspaper, it has to be today," Taylor told Brian Hilliard early the next morning. "After that, I've got other work obligations."

"No problem. Hang on while I check my calendar."

Taylor heard the clack of the computer keyboard on the other end of the phone line.

"Can we do it at noon here at the paper? That way Krista

Sue could be here, too, if you don't mind. I know she had some questions for you, too."

Taylor wasn't surprised. It seemed a lot of people harbored secret aspirations to write something someday. She was happy to share whatever knowledge she had. "No problem. I'll see you then."

Taylor arrived at the Laramie newspaper office promptly at noon. Brian was already there, seated behind the editor's desk in the small newsroom. He got up from his desk as she approached and reached across to shake her hand. "Krista Sue isn't here yet."

"That's okay." Taylor sat down in the chair he indicated. "Do you want to wait?"

Brian pursed his lips. "I'm thinking we should—if only to avoid going over some of the same material twice."

"No problem," Taylor said, recalling what Krista Sue had said about her fiance's impatient nature.

"While we're waiting, I have a question for you, of a business nature," he said. He picked up a pencil, twisted it in his hands.

Taylor set her shoulder bag on the floor beside her. "Fire away."

Brian leaned forward. "I'm sure you know that newspapers are fast being eclipsed by the Internet these days. Most are really struggling financially and we're no exception here. The thing is, the Internet tends to focus on national and international news. The local stuff that is of interest to the people in the individual communities isn't covered with the same energy and commitment it once was. So I think papers can still serve a need, plus possibly grow, if the material inside the paper is interesting enough. Which brings me to my pitch. I would like you to consider writing a weekly column for us, talking about the plight of the twenty-something woman, all the issues they face. It could be funny and poignant...anything you want. And the great thing is, if it's a hit here, we might be able to get you syndicated in a lot of other small community papers. In Texas alone, there are hundreds that might be interested in what you have to say, and that could add up for you financially." He told her what he would be willing to pay, per column and had her multiply that by ten other newspapers.

Taylor did the math. "I'm stunned."

"I can see that." He smiled. "In a good way, I hope."

"Yes. Absolutely." If this worked out the way they both hoped, it could be the answer to all her financial problems, give her more of a steady income while she wrote her novels.

Before they could continue negotiations, Krista Sue rushed in, perspiring and out of breath. "I'm so sorry, Brian," she said. "I was working on lesson plans—the principal wants me to have a whole year's worth ready by August first, since I've never taught school here before, and it is taking forever! I got so frustrated I decided to work on my sewing for a while and then time got away from me."

Clearly exasperated with the reason behind his fiancée's tardiness, Brian got to his feet. "Tell me you didn't take it apart again."

"It's not right! I know how I want it to look but I just can't get it there, not yet anyway." Krista Sue gave Brian a one-armed hug and stood on tiptoe to kiss his cheek. "I'm really sorry," she said, looking at that moment so totally in love with her husband-to-be it made Taylor's heart ache. "Forgive me? Please?"

"Of course." Brian looked completely smitten with Krista Sue, too. "But it's Taylor here you should be apologizing to."

"I'm sorry." Krista Sue dropped into a chair beside Taylor. "I didn't mean to keep you waiting."

"No problem." Luckily for Taylor, Zak Townsend hadn't

arrived in Texas and commanded Taylor's presence on the set—yet.

"So let's get to it." Brian pulled up a list of questions on his laptop computer screen.

"What I want to know," Krista Sue said when Brian had concluded his interview, "is how you found the courage to go after that career when your family and everyone else expected that you would do something completely different, like become a doctor."

"It wasn't easy," Taylor admitted, looking first at Krista Sue, then at Brian, who suddenly had the funniest look on his face.

"What?" Taylor asked.

"I just Googled you," Brian said.

Uh-oh. "And?" Taylor asked warily.

He shook his head, still staring at the screen. "You're not going to believe what just came up."

TAYLOR FOUND Jeremy in the hospital cafeteria, having lunch with Paige and a few other young doctors. It was clear from the surprised but completely unsuspecting expression on his face that he had no clue what was awaiting them. She said hello to everyone, chatted briefly, then said, "I've got to talk to you. Alone."

"Whoo-hooo," the group teased in unison.

Jeremy shrugged, accepting the request like the big, studly guy he was. "When duty calls," he winked. He grabbed what was left of his sandwich, and his iced tea, then deposited his tray in the tray-return next to the door. "Have you had lunch? Can I get you something?"

"No. And no."

"Where do you want to do this? Outside?"

"Your private office. We need a computer with Internet access."

"Curious and curiouser, but I'm in." He finished his sandwich in two bites and continued walking. "You look awfully pretty today."

Taylor blushed self-consciously. "Thanks."

"How'd the interview go at the newspaper?" Jeremy asked.

Taylor winced. "That's what we have to talk about."

"You're being especially mysterious." He crossed over to the annex, where the doctors' offices were located, via the connecting covered walkway.

"Trust me." Taylor sighed. "It's something you just have to see."

Short minutes later, they were in Jeremy's private office, with the door closed. Taylor motioned toward his desk. "May I?" When Jeremy nodded his assent, Taylor took his chair and Googled her name.

The very first thing that came up was a link to The Celebrity Dish Web site. At the top of the page was a series of photos. Jeremy looked. Blinked. Swore. "My feelings exactly," Taylor said with heartfelt emotion.

"That's—"

"Me taking off my T-shirt and capris by the swimming pool the night I arrived."

Jeremy moved in for a closer look. "The way these photos are arranged, it makes you look like you're doing a strip tease."

Taylor leaned back in the chair. "Keep scrolling. It gets better."

He swore again, more virulently this time. "That's me."

She nodded. "Lounging back against the side of the pool with what looks like a tropical lagoon behind you. I especially love that expectant, sultry, give-it-to-me smile on your face."

He turned to look at her. "Anyone ever tell you that you can be too descriptive?"

"Keep going."

Jeremy did and swore again.

"Yep," Taylor concluded out loud, continuing her play-by-play. "There's me, diving in, swimming over to you."

Jeremy frowned and dragged a chair over so he could sit down next to her. "It looks like we're flirting."

"And then some," Taylor observed with a shake of her head. "But it gets even better."

Jeremy groaned and playfully covered his eyes with his palm. "I'm afraid to look."

She wished she hadn't. But she had, so… "Then I'll scroll for you." She moved to the next set of photos. "And there you are, coming out of the pool. In all your naked glory. Chasing that fan who was obviously not a fan but a tabloid photographer."

"Well, at least the tabloid put a black bar across my most private parts. I wish they'd done the same with my butt."

So did Taylor. She'd never really studied it before, the way the pictures enticed her to peruse it. He had a really cute butt. Nice back and shoulders, too. Powerful thighs, arms, everything really. Not that she should be concentrating on that.

"And then the last frame." Instructing herself to ignore the tingling sensations rushing through her limbs, she scrolled to the last page. Taylor was standing there in her dripping wet underwear, clearly chilled, facing Jeremy. Her hand cupping his bicep, she had her face turned up to his. He was gazing down at her. It looked like they were lovers all right.

Jeremy scrolled back to the top, then all the way through, pausing over the photos of her in dishabille the same way she had ruminated over his. "It looks like you stripped for me, dove in and swam over to me. Then I apparently chased you out of the pool, until we caught each other."

"The inference being that we then made love."

He sat back, frowning. "Well, we know that's not true."

"The point is, you're now in the middle of this scandal with me, since you have been erroneously identified as another one of my lovers."

His glance drifted over her. "How many are there?"

She returned his amused look. "Very funny."

He stood and dismissed the budding scandal with a shake of his head. "No one's going to believe this. Heck, no one is even going to know about it."

Taylor stood, too. "You're fooling yourself if you really think that. The public eats this stuff up, Jeremy."

He shrugged, unconcerned. "It doesn't matter what people we don't know think. We'll tell those we do know what happened and that will be that."

"You really think it will be that simple?"

He gave her a reassuring smile and a pat on the shoulder. "I do."

"TALK ABOUT a one-horse town!" Zak Townsend complained, taking a seat opposite Taylor in the Lone Star Dance Hall. At seven-thirty on Friday evening, the popular restaurant was bustling with activity. Trays of sumptuous Texas-style food were being brought out to the filled tables. Country music played on the sound system. Couples were two-stepping on the dance floor. Taylor hadn't wanted to meet there to discuss the script changes, but Zak had been adamant, so here she was, pen and notepad in front of her.

"Where's Zoe?" Taylor asked, knowing the rock diva was bound to have her own list of proposed story changes, too.

"In that dive they call the best inn in Laramie." Zak settled back in his chair. Like Taylor, he was dressed in jeans, western shirt, boots—although his were obviously couture. Which made him appear more pretentious than ever.

"Can you believe it?" he continued, grumbling irritably. "They had a vending machine area instead of a restaurant."

"I think that's because there are a dozen fine restaurants just down the street, all within easy walking distance."

"Naturally, there's no room service."

"Any of the restaurants in town will deliver to the inn for a small fee."

"No sauna. No tennis or racquetball courts. An outdoor pool. When we checked in, I thought Zoe was going to cry."

I'll bet.

"Have you ever stayed there?"

"Yes." Taylor had found the rooms clean and comfortable, outfitted with everything—including cable television and high speed Internet connections—a patron might reasonably need.

"We've booked you a room there, too, by the way," Zak added.

Taylor ignored the subtle come-on in his expression. "I have a place to stay. Thanks."

"It would be easier for us to go over the changes, if you were there, too."

Like hell it would. "We can do it by phone and e-mail."

He looked her up and down with a familiarity that rankled. "You still haven't forgiven me for that little kiss, have you?"

It hadn't exactly been a kiss. He'd gone in for one, but Taylor had seen it coming and turned her head away in the nick of time. She hadn't been able to get away from him immediately because of the iron grip he'd had on her shoulder and waist. But a painful jab to his instep had fixed that. Unfortunately, however, she hadn't been able to break free before their photo had been taken.

"Are we going to talk about the changes or not?" Taylor asked.

The waitress, a college girl in T-shirt and jeans, stopped at their table. "Have you folks had a chance to look at the menu?" she asked politely.

"I've already had dinner," Taylor fibbed, anxious to get their business over with and get out of there, "but I'll have an iced tea."

Zak perused the menu, then snapped it shut. "I'll have the grilled salmon, rare, and a double bourbon and branch."

"That comes with a salad and choice of side—"

"No thanks. I'd sooner pour saturated fat directly into my vein."

Ignoring Zak's rude tone, the waitress wrote down the order, took the menu with a tolerant smile, and headed off.

"You might try being a little nicer," Taylor advised, knowing Zak's sarcasm would soon be making the rounds of the kitchen.

"She didn't even know who I was. No one here seems to recognize me."

In an effort to stave off further unpleasantness, Taylor corrected, "I'm sure they all do."

Zak appeared to consider that. "Then why aren't they gawking and asking for my autograph?"

"Because they are used to having stars in their midst. Beau Chamberlain built his film studio here twenty-eight years ago. Dozens of films have been made there over the years. One of the reasons actors and directors like coming to Laramie is the way they are treated when they are here. The residents of Laramie respect a celebrity's privacy every bit as much as they prize their own."

"That's…weird."

"It's nice. If you like a quiet life." And Taylor, who'd grown up in the hustle and bustle of Dallas, did. "So what did you have in mind for the new material?" she asked.

Immediately enthused, Zak relayed, "My character goes out to the desert because he has decided he needs a change of pace. Zoe's character is stifling my creativity. I'm thinking that I—he—should take a guitar and write a song while he's out in the desert. In any case, he finds this beautiful Indian woman and they're really hot for each other, so they get it on—"

"You've got to be joking! I'm not writing infidelity into this script. It will kill the romance!" What little was left of it.

"A good writer can make even the most fantastic plot twist work, same as any actor, as long as you feel it in here." Zak grabbed Taylor's hand and plastered it over his heart, as if to demonstrate.

Furious, Taylor pulled free of his tight grasp. "Do not do that again!"

"You need to loosen up." Zak stood, grasped Taylor's wrist, and yanked her onto the dance floor. A lively country tune was playing. One of his hands clamped the back of her waist, the other locked on her right wrist.

Taylor smiled, trying not to make even more of a scene. "I don't want to do this, Zak. I want to get back to work and get out of here."

"Too bad. I'm the boss…I call the shots." Zak let go of his grip on her waist and twirled her around.

That suddenly, Taylor saw Jeremy coming toward her. So did Zak, who was so stunned, he temporarily let go of Taylor's wrist.

Looking handsome as ever in jeans, a white western shirt and straw hat, Jeremy latched on and danced Taylor away from the egomaniacal actor. "Seems like I got here just in the nick of time," Jeremy whispered in her ear.

Taylor was grateful for the interruption. She did not, however, need it. "I can take care of myself," she said flatly, wresting free of Jeremy's grip, too.

The waitress was suddenly right there, hand to Taylor's arm. "You may not have noticed, but there is a lady over there who just came in a couple of minutes ago, and she's been taking pictures of you and Mr. Townsend."

Taylor turned. So did Jeremy. They saw the same fifty-something blonde who'd photographed them poolside on the Chamberlain ranch, dressed in sneakers and a plain blue chambray dress, suitable for a PTA meeting this time.

"We can ask her to leave if you like," the waitress said.

"What's the problem?" Zak wanted to know.

"Papparazzi." Jeremy started for the interloper responsible for the pictures of his bare butt. The woman snapped one more quick photo of the three of them and then took off. Camera still in hand, she threaded her way through patrons, knocking into tables, bumping waitstaff, causing a whole tray of drinks to go flying.

Jeremy was right after her, with Taylor close behind.

She had just made it through the double restaurant doors, onto the concrete porch that fronted the popular nightspot, when Zak grabbed her. "Stop right now!" he yelled at Jeremy. "Or Taylor pays!"

THE SCENE WAS SO movielike and so ludicrous, Jeremy didn't know whether to laugh or give Zak Townsend a punch that would send the self-righteous prig flying to the ground.

Not about to let him threaten Taylor in any way, Jeremy gave up chasing the woman they now knew was a paparazzo and went back to Zak. "You've got one second to take your hands off of her or I rearrange your face."

Zak let go. "Calm down. It was a joke."

Taylor looked at Jeremy. "That was the trespasser from the other night! I think she is following me."

Zak scoffed, "Why would she be doing that?"

"Because she's profiting from these ridiculous rumors about a romance between me and you!" Taylor glared at Zak.

"So?" Zak looked bored again. "What does it matter what the tabloids print? You can't stop 'em, so you may as well ignore them."

Jeremy interjected himself between Taylor and Zak. "Plenty of celebrities do stop them with a lawsuit."

"Well, not me," Zak vowed, "and not Zoe. We are not going to war with the press…and I would advise you, if you know what is good for you, not to do so, either. Now if you don't mind—" Zak started to reach for Taylor yet again.

"Actually," Jeremy said, "I do." Sensing she needed rescuing even if she didn't admit to it, he wrapped his arm around Taylor's waist. Ignoring the vibration of anger flowing through her slender frame, he leaned down to whisper in her ear, "Remember, sweetheart, we've got that thing tonight with Kevin McCabe?"

"Oh." Taylor got the hint. "Yes."

Zak was about to interrupt again, when he saw Zoe and her bevy of personal assistants coming down the street. Zak turned to Taylor. "I'll expect the new scenes by tomorrow morning."

The restaurant doors opened and their waitress came out. She had Taylor's shoulder bag and notebook and pen in hand. "I wasn't sure if you-all were leaving or what," she said, handing Taylor's belongings to her, before turning back to Zak. "But your salmon and bourbon are ready…."

"I'll be right in." Zak wrapped his arm around his wife, as if Zoe were the love of his life. After a brief exchange of very telling looks, Zoe's entourage broke-up and headed on up the street, to have dinner elsewhere.

To Jeremy's satisfaction, Taylor did not resist as Jeremy put his arm around her waist. They walked to his pickup truck in the crowded parking lot. "So who is Kevin McCabe?" she asked finally.

"A friend and a detective with the Laramie County Sheriff's Department," Jeremy said. "Our privacy has been invaded. We're going to put a stop to it."

Luckily for them, Kevin was on duty that evening. The down-to-earth lawman listened to what Taylor and Jeremy had to say, laughed when he saw the photos of his old friend, Jeremy's, bare butt on The Celebrity Dish Web site, and frowned when he heard the woman had been snapping pictures of them again that evening.

"Zak Townsend is correct," Kevin told them. "She had as much right as you-all to be in the restaurant this evening."

"So even if we'd gotten her camera—" Jeremy theorized.

"You can't take her film. Not without risking she'll file charges against you. You can sue her for posting photos of the two of you on the Internet without your permission but that takes time and money. Lots of money. These tabloid magazines have a lot of lawyers and very deep pockets."

Jeremy refused to back down. "Can we press charges for her trespassing on the Chamberlain ranch Monday night?"

Kevin set down his pen. "If we can identify the paparazzo, and Paige or her parents agree to press charges, sure. The problem is, without a license plate or some kind of photo, it's going to be hard to identify her and track her down. If you see her again, acting illegally or stalking you, and you can let us know, we can certainly bring her in for questioning, see if she has any other outstanding complaints or warrants against her. At that point, you could probably get the court to issue a restraining order against her. But all that is going to take time. Realistically, she's probably already e-mailed the photos she took tonight to another gossip rag."

"Thanks for your help." Jeremy stood and shook Kevin's hand.

"No problem. Just wish I could do more." Kevin walked them out.

Jeremy and Taylor stood on the curb in front of the sheriff's station.

He was about to ask her something when the door to the Laramie newspaper office opened, across the street.

Brian Hilliard came out, waving wildly. "Doc!" he yelled. "Come quick!"

Chapter Six

Nervous Studio Considers Canceling Film

The industry buzz surrounding Zak and Zoe Townsend's first film remains grim. Execs who have seen the rough cut of *Sail Away* declare it an unmitigated mess. Much of the blame is being shifted to the script, written by first-time novelist Taylor O'Quinn, who is now rumored to be romantically involved with Zak Townsend. Last-minute efforts to save the beleaguered project are said to be underway….

Entertainment News Update
Cable News Channel, June 6

Jeremy raced across the street and Taylor was right behind him.

"Hurry!" Brian Hilliard held the door to the Laramie newspaper office. "There's something wrong with Krista Sue!"

Indeed, there was, Taylor noted. The young woman was bent over in a chair, sweating furiously, trying to get her breath.

"Get a paper bag!" Jeremy said.

Brian looked around frantically, finally fishing a sack that had held someone's takeout order, out of the trash. He dumped the contents into the can, handed it over.

Jeremy fit the top around Krista Sue's mouth. "Breathe into this. Nice and easy. That's it. Keep going. You're doing good."

Slowly but surely, Krista Sue began to recover. Only then did Brian finally relax.

Eventually, Jeremy was able to ease the paper bag away from her face. "Thank you," Krista Sue said. Tears of what Taylor assumed were embarrassment glittered in her eyes. "I don't know what happened. I was just sitting here, waiting on Brian to finish so we could go to dinner, and working on my lesson plans for next year, when all of a sudden I got dizzy and my chest started feeling really tight and I couldn't get my breath!" Fresh tears rolled down her cheeks.

"When was the last time you ate?" Jeremy asked.

Krista Sue gestured vaguely. "I'm not sure. Noon, maybe. Quite a while ago."

Jeremy looked at Brian. "Do you have any orange juice or anything?"

"I can go get some."

"Why don't you do that?" Jeremy said. "Taylor and I will stay here with Krista Sue."

After Brian took off, Jeremy pulled up two chairs while Taylor spotted a box of tissues and handed it to Krista Sue. The young woman sniffed gratefully and dabbed at the tears still streaming from her eyes. Thinking this was a medical problem, best handled between patient and doctor, Taylor offered quietly, "You know I can wait outside if you two would like to talk privately."

"I'd like you to stay." Krista Sue swallowed hard and continued with a self-effacing laugh, "It isn't every evening I make such a complete fool of myself."

"I know we don't know each other all that well yet."

Jeremy regarded her compassionately. "I've only been your family doc for the last six weeks. But I'd like to help."

"And you can't do that unless I tell you what is going on with me." Krista Sue twisted the tissue in her hands.

Jeremy nodded. "Does it have anything to do with your wedding?"

"No. I love Brian very much. I want to marry him. What I don't want to do is teach school." Krista Sue cried all the harder. Brushing the moisture away with the heel of her hand, she looked at Taylor. "That's why I wanted to talk to you, to ask you how you got the courage to take a different career path when everyone was pushing you into something you knew wasn't right for you."

Taylor's heart went out to the young woman. "It wasn't easy. But I felt better when I told everyone the truth." Taylor brought her chair closer. "Do you have any idea what you do want to do?"

Krista Sue flashed a watery smile. "I'd like to sew clothing for a living. Not design it—I don't have the creativity for that— but I love making things fit really well on someone."

Taylor surveyed the white eyelet creation Krista Sue had on. "Did you make that sundress?"

"Yes. I started with a basic pattern and then kept ripping it apart and redoing it until I got the fit just right."

She'd done an amazing job. The dress was just beautiful.

"Why don't you ask my aunt Jenna for a job?" Jeremy asked.

Krista Sue wouldn't find a better teacher, Taylor knew. Jenna Lockhart Remington was famous for her custom wedding dresses and evening gowns, as well as her line of off-the-rack evening wear. Her couture boutique was located right there in Laramie, on Main Street. The factory that made her department-store dresses was located in Laramie, too.

"I can't do that." Krista Sue blew her nose. "I don't have any training."

"Maybe you could do an internship," Taylor suggested.

A wistful light came into Krista Sue's eyes. "Internships pay very little. Brian just poured every last cent he inherited from his grandfather into purchasing the newspaper. I know he'll make a success of it, but in the meantime we're going to need my income as a teacher to live on. I can't let him down. No, like it or not, I'm just going to have to follow through on my word, shelve my own dreams, and start teaching school in the fall."

"I OWE YOU ONE for finally getting the truth out of Krista Sue," Jeremy told Taylor minutes later, as they left the newspaper while an unsuspecting Brian Hilliard tended to his fiancée. "I've been trying to get Krista Sue to open up to me for weeks. She wouldn't do it—not until tonight, and I think she only did it then because you were there, too."

"Don't give me too much credit," Taylor said, "Krista Sue only confided in me because she read my book, and knows I've been where she is." Taylor paused at the corner, waiting for the traffic light to change. "It's really hard to take a career path when everyone who knows and loves you is telling you not to do it."

Jeremy turned his glance away from all the evening traffic. "I really hurt you."

"It's over." Taylor shrugged and started across the street.

"It's still not right." Jeremy moved in close, as pedestrians passed to his left. "I should have supported you." He caught her elbow in a light, protective grasp.

Taylor's arm tingled, long after they reached the opposite sidewalk, and he dropped his hold on her once again. Stepping back under the awning of the antique shop, she said, "You're supporting me now."

Jeremy met her eyes. He stood, his back to the flow of on-lookers, both on foot and in vehicles cruising past on Main Street. "Why are you suddenly so willing to let me off the hook?"

She hadn't been a week ago, she knew. Emotions in turmoil, Taylor shrugged. "Maybe because we've both grown up since then." Because a lot more had been going on between them back then—that had taken her years to realize. "And because I see how futile it is to hold on to old grudges and hurts when there's a present-day friendship to be had between us."

Jeremy grinned and began strolling down the street again, toward the place where they'd parked their vehicles. "I like the sound of that."

"Good. Well…I guess I…" She glanced toward her Jeep, wishing the evening didn't have to end.

"Have you had dinner yet?"

Taylor looked up at him. "No."

"Neither have I." He indicated the park, half a block up, opposite the town square. "Up for a picnic?"

Taylor worked to rein in her feelings. "As long as it occurs back at the Chamberlain ranch, only lasts long enough for us to eat, *and* you realize it's not a date."

Not the least bit dissuaded by her numerous conditions, he said, "I know that I have to wait until the septic system and heating and air-conditioning are put in."

He said it with such good humor she had trouble stifling a chuckle.

His expression full of that steely determination she knew so well, he continued, "It's happening this weekend, by the way."

Taylor's breath stalled halfway up her windpipe. "What?"

"The installation—of both."

"How did you manage that?" Taylor asked.

"I told both men that you wouldn't go out with me until the work was done."

She didn't know whether to be embarrassed or thrilled. In truth, she felt a little of each. "You didn't!"

"I did." He grinned proudly. "And they took pity on me, too." He shook his head in exaggerated confoundment. "Neither of them imagined doctors could be so hard up for dates."

Taylor chided, "You're not hard up."

"Only for the woman I want," he agreed, a twinkle in his eyes. "But not to worry. I'm going to get there."

And then what? Taylor wondered. Would circumstances outside the realm of their feelings come between them once again? "You may be singing a different tune when everyone in town learns you're being dragged into this brouhaha with me and the Townsends," she warned. Bad enough she was in this tabloid scandal mess, without dragging anyone else in with her.

Jeremy shrugged. "Everyone already knows. Nobody cares. They know me and they know the veracity of those rags."

Taylor chewed on her lower lip. "You won't lose any patients over this?"

"None I'd want to keep. Seriously, Taylor, Laramie is a great place to live and work. The people here know what's important."

His support enveloped her in warmth. "And what is that?"

He caught both her hands in his, tightened his fingers over hers. "Family, friends, satisfying work. A place to hang your hat at the end of the day."

He had no idea how good that sounded to her, after years away from her home state. "Like Lago Vista Ranch." She guessed where his hope centered.

One corner of Jeremy's mouth crooked up ruefully. "Or The Gentleman Rancher's Folly, as some around here have been known to call it."

TO SAY TAYLOR WAS DISTRACTED during their "picnic" back at the Chamberlain ranch was an understatement. She lost track of the conversation more times than he could count. Jeremy recognized the faraway look in her eyes, and knew whatever was absorbing her so thoroughly was work-related. He behaved that way himself when mulling over a medical case that was particularly thorny.

Predictably, no sooner had they wolfed down their takeout grilled chicken salads and pecan pie out by the pool, than she was standing again. "Thanks so much for the dinner. That was really good."

"And now…?"

She flashed him a grateful smile. "Gotta go."

Jeremy helped gather up the trash. "It's still early—only ten." And while this might not be a date…it was Friday night. He enjoyed hanging out with her. Being near her after so much time apart.

Regret flashed in her blue eyes. "It's early if you want to go to bed. Not so early if you've got three new scenes due first thing tomorrow morning." Stress tautened the lines of her face. "That's what I was doing with Zak tonight—getting my assignment."

Aware how pretty she looked in the soft outdoor lighting, Jeremy walked with her toward the ranch house.

Jeremy would do whatever possible to ease the tension from her brow. "How about I make you a pot of coffee?"

"Thanks, but I've had enough caffeine from the tea to keep me up all night." She sauntered away from him, hands in the pockets of her jeans, then turned back and said over her shoulder, "Good luck tomorrow with all the stuff going on at your ranch!"

Jeremy nodded. "To you, too—with your writing." Appreciating the sight of her, so lovely and intent, Jeremy watched her disappear into the ranch house. Minutes later, she had her laptop out on the kitchen table. He could see her through the windows, sitting with a thoughtful expression on her face, her hands poised over the keyboard.

Body aching in places it had no business aching, Jeremy went back to his bedroom, found the swim trunks he'd neglected to use the other night, and put them on. An hour of laps later, he was no closer to being sleepy. A warm shower didn't help. Ignoring the urge to wander out to the ranch house kitchen and engage Taylor in more banter, he picked up her book and read the blurb. *No one understands being on the rebound better than Taylor O'Quinn.* What, Jeremy wondered, did Taylor know about that? Who had broken her heart…to the point she'd felt compelled to write a novel about it?

THE PINK AND YELLOW LIGHTS of dawn streaked across the edge of pale gray sky. Taylor stepped out onto the patio, cup of coffee in hand. It was her fifth of the night, as it happened. She'd had to make not one—but two—pots of coffee after all.

"Get it all done?" a low voice asked behind her.

Taylor turned. Jeremy had on an old T-shirt and jeans. He hadn't shaved. His hair had that sexy, rumpled, just out of bed on a Saturday morning, can't bother with a comb look. He had a pair of sunglasses in one hand, a set of keys in the other. Her heart skipped a beat at the sight of him.

After setting her mug down, she walked closer. "I just e-mailed the pages in. I'm about to go to bed." She stretched her arms above her head, easing the stiffness from her body, then just as slowly put them back down. She looked into his eyes. He looked well-rested and ready for action. "Where are you headed?"

"The ranch. I'm not on call this weekend, so I'm going to be doing some work out there, while the installation guys are there."

And she'd thought it would never happen. "I'm impressed."

His dark brown eyes lit up. "Yeah?"

"That ranch is your dream. You *should* do everything you can to make it a reality so you can start living out there."

Intimacy simmered between them. "Thanks for the push," he told her in a gruff tone.

Taylor swallowed around the sudden dryness in her throat. "I'm sure I'm not the first."

"You're the only one I've listened to, oddly enough. So back to that date you owe me…" Jeremy took the opening with the single-mindedness he was known for. "I know it can't happen until the work on the ranch is done, and that's going to take a couple days, but we could still hang out together while that's happening. Play some putt-putt, grab a bite. Right?"

Taylor knew they were headed into dangerous territory. They'd just resurrected their friendship. Seeing each other socially, if it didn't work out, could hamper that. She did not want Jeremy to fade from her life again. He meant too much to her. So if that meant playing it safe… "We could ask Paige to come along, too. She loves putt-putt golf."

Jeremy appeared amenable. "That'd be great except she went to Lubbock to attend a wedding this weekend, remember?"

There went their chaperone. "Oh, yeah."

Jeremy moved in. "What about tonight? Are you busy?"

Taylor tilted her head back and gazed up at him. "I could meet you in town around seven or so, whenever I'm finished."

His brow furrowed. "What's going on there?"

"I telephoned your aunt Jenna last night, on the drive back here, and asked her if she would be willing to talk to Krista Sue about a career as a couture seamstress, at least clue her into what is involved before she gives up on her secret aspiration. She said yes, so Krista Sue and I are meeting your aunt at her salon at six o'clock."

"You're going all out to help Krista Sue," Jeremy said, admiration in his gaze.

Taylor shrugged. "I know how hard it is to pursue something most people would view as a pipe dream. Once you have success as an actor, writer, or artist, you get all kinds of respect. While you're trying to make it happen…it's not so straightforward. It's pretty easy to doubt yourself. Krista Sue obviously has a talent for dressmaking. I'd like to see her use it, rather than stick to a more conventional path that is not going to make her—or those around her—happy."

"She's lucky to have you in her corner."

"I haven't done anything yet, except arrange a meeting." Taylor just hoped it went as well as she envisioned.

Jeremy left and Taylor went on to bed. She awakened around four, refreshed, and hopped in the shower. Telling herself it didn't matter what she wore since this was not a date, she put on the first casual cotton skirt she came across in her suitcase, cropped shirt and sandals. Deciding that looked a little plain, she added a necklace and earrings, and a spritz of perfume. Then she drove to town.

Krista Sue met her in the parking area behind the dress salon. "I'm really nervous."

"Relax. Jenna is really nice."

Krista Sue fell into step beside her. "How do you know her?"

Together, they walked through the shady alley that led to historic Main Street. "Jenna likes to use girl-next-door types instead of professional clotheshorses to market her off-the-rack designs to department stores, so my friend Paige and I both modeled for her while we were in college."

Jenna was waiting for them when they entered her boutique. Although the striking redhead now had salons on Rodeo Drive in Beverly Hills and on Fifth Avenue in New York City, this remained her flagship store, same as it had during the days when Jenna was just getting started and lived in the apartment above the salon. "Hi, Jenna." Taylor hugged the woman who had unwittingly been Taylor's mentor in so many ways.

"Good to see you again." Jenna hugged her back, looking svelte and pretty in a black and white wrap dress of her own creation.

Krista Sue and Jenna shook hands. Jenna led them over to the comfortable semi-circular sofa in the main salon. Slowly but surely Jenna coaxed Krista Sue to tell her how she had learned to sew as a child, and had always loved it, although she had no interest in design. "What fascinates me is the actual sewing of a garment, trying to make it fit just so."

Jenna took in Krista Sue's dress. "You made the dress you're wearing, didn't you?"

Krista Sue nodded. Jenna smiled. "You did a beautiful job on it."

"Thank you."

"To work for me as a seamstress, you'd need to complete an apprenticeship in the salon, here in Laramie," Jenna told Krista Sue. "Unfortunately, I don't have any openings just now. I am, however, looking for a new sales associate here in the shop. The job comes with full benefits. Are you interested in auditioning for the position?"

JEREMY PARKED in front of the Jenna Lockhart salon and got out. Through the big picture window he saw a most perplexing sight. Taylor was standing on the pedestal in front of the three-way mirror, clad in a white satin gown that might have been all right for some woman but was definitely all wrong for her. Krista Sue was helping her put on a veil that was even more over-the-top ridiculous for someone as down-to-earth as Taylor. Worse, Taylor seemed to be throwing some sort of hissy fit.

Curious, Jeremy went in. His aunt Jenna turned to him with a warning look. She slid her bifocals down her nose. "You can stay if you sit down and don't say a word until we are done," she hissed to him.

He held up his hands in surrender, mouthing, "All right."

Jenna glared at him, further commanding him to silence.

Taylor caught sight of Jeremy in the mirror. She turned to him, flushing brightly, holding the ridiculously frilly gown against her breasts.

"Honestly, I think we can do much better than this," Krista Sue told Taylor gently.

"This is the one I want!" Taylor stamped her foot. "I've always dreamed of a dress with poofy sleeves and a headdress veil!"

Ignoring Jenna Lockhart's watchful eye, Krista Sue stepped back and said with the kind of excellent service all shoppers wished for, "The dress can definitely be cut down to size." She took several pins and demonstrated, by bringing in the fabric around Taylor's slender waist and full breasts, and securing the fabric in a way that completely transformed the formerly too-big garment. "But I think you might want to try—just for comparison—something with more simple, elegant lines. If you don't like it," Krista Sue promised deferentially, "we'll take it right off."

"Well…" Taylor pouted, ignoring Jeremy's eyes.

"It'll be worth the time and effort," Krista Sue soothed. "You'll see."

"All right!" Behaving like a spoiled princess, Taylor flounced out, skirt in both hands. Looking eager yet determined, Krista Sue glided after her.

"What's going on?" Jeremy demanded of his aunt, as soon as the two young women had disappeared into the adjacent dressing room.

Jenna relaxed. "Taylor is being 'the exceedingly difficult client.' Krista Sue is auditioning for a job as saleswoman."

"Ah." Jeremy paused.

Jenna read his mind. "For the record, that first dress was not mine. We use it as a test to see how well a potential sales-woman can pin, to give a client an idea how nicely the dress will look once we're done with the custom fit."

His aunt studied him over the rim of her stylish bifocals. "What are you doing here?"

"Looking for Taylor," Jeremy admitted.

She tried to contain a smile. "Oh?"

"We're just hanging out."

"I see."

It was too soon for anyone else to be jumping to conclu-sions when he didn't even know where his relationship with Taylor was actually going to end up. Although he knew what he *wanted* to happen between them.

The two women came back out, and Taylor stepped up on the pedestal. This time, she was definitely in one of Jenna's designs. The strapless gown hugged her midriff like a second skin, the skirt fluffed out around her hips. The veil Krista Sue selected had a plain satin band that fit like a headband on Taylor's gorgeous black hair. She looked incredible, Jeremy thought. She looked like a bride. So much so that he could imagine standing next to the minister, waiting—and watching—as she glided down the aisle toward him on her father's arm.

Wondering where that thought had come from—he shook it off. Just in time to see Taylor's lower lip slide out petulantly once again. "I don't like it," she said, stomping her foot. "It makes me look fat! And plain!"

To her credit, Krista Sue did not even blink. She merely placated Taylor in an understanding tone and went to the rack to select another gown and veil. And then another and another and another. Until nearly an hour and a half had gone by and Taylor finally found one that had pleased her.

JEREMY OFFERED TO CLOSE UP for his aunt, while she walked out with Krista Sue.

He was just getting ready to switch off the showroom lights when Taylor came rushing out, purse in one hand, sandals in the other. "Sorry that took so long." She paused next to the sales counter and bent to put her shoes on.

Jeremy grinned, taking in her shapely legs. "No problem," he teased. "I enjoyed the show."

Straightening, she tugged her knee-length skirt down over her hips. "No need to be kind."

Jeremy hit the switch. The showroom was bathed in the dusky light of early evening. "Who's being kind?" They walked towards the long hall that led to the salon's service entrance. Taylor had looked incredible in one gown after another. He fell into step beside her, adjusting his strides to her smaller steps. "I never got why guys went shopping with their girlfriends. Now I know."

"Somehow I never figured you for a fashionista."

"There's a lot you don't know about me."

Taylor sized him up. "I'm beginning to think so." She paused. "It went well tonight, don't you think?"

Happy his aunt had offered Krista Sue a job as a salesclerk, Jeremy predicted, "I think that's one patient I'm going to be seeing a lot less often in the office."

"Let's hope so." Taylor headed for the exit. "What would you like to do next?"

Jeremy plucked a white satin thread from her hair and held it aloft. "Pick out flowers for the wedding?"

She frowned at the stray thread. "Very funny, cowboy."

"Seriously," Jeremy paused next to the electronic panel that controlled the salon's security system, "you looked amazing in all those dresses."

Taylor assessed his veracity with pretty blue eyes. "And you didn't look all that bored."

He hadn't been. In fact, watching her prance around in those designer wedding gowns had thrown him for a loop. Before he realized what he was implying, he blurted out, "You're going to be a beautiful bride one day, Taylor."

Chapter Seven

Ultimatum!

Screenwriter Taylor O'Quinn has had enough of The
Other Woman status! Now she's threatening to marry
her former/current(?!?) lover, Texas doctor Jeremy
Carrigan, if Zak Townsend doesn't deliver a divorce
decree from spouse Zoe—and a ring and a proposal to
his demanding mistress very soon! Not that she is an
easy woman to please, in any case, as evidenced by her
foot-stamping hissy fit in the ultra-chic Jenna Lockhart
salon. Seems the smitten doc watched her try on dozens
of wedding dresses and veils, before she found one to
her liking….

Celeb Page, *The New York Daily Express*
June 7

Taylor folded her arms in front of her. She regarded Jeremy
like an armadillo who had wandered in from outside. "Since
when are *you* so sentimental?"

Jeremy slanted her a mocking look. "Hey, even I have my
Hallmark moments." Then he winked, clearly attempting to

lighten the mood. "But let's keep this to ourselves, OK? I have a reputation to uphold, after all."

Unnerved by the personal nature of the conversation, Taylor braced her spine against the wall of the narrow corridor. "Well, since we're exchanging niceties, I'm sure you'll be a handsome groom one day," Taylor retorted.

Jeremy reactivated the security system via the panel in the back hallway, opened the back door, and ushered her out into the alley. Hand cupping her elbow, he led her toward the front of the building where his pickup truck was parked. "Have you ever thought about tying the knot?" He opened the passenger door. "Say…to Baywatch Bart?"

She climbed into the passenger seat. "We were never engaged."

Jeremy sat behind the wheel and drove the short distance to the Armadillo Acres miniature golf course. "Were you ever betrothed to anyone else?"

Taylor looked at Jeremy. "Why do you ask?"

He shrugged and came around to help her with her door. "You seem to know a lot about being on the rebound."

Yes, Taylor thought, she did know what it felt like to have her heart broken, her hope crushed. Together, they headed for the ticket office, and Jeremy paid the admission fee. The clerk handed them two clubs, a couple of golf balls, and a scoring sheet and pencil. As soon as they were through the gates, Taylor picked up where the conversation had left off. "You know what my novel was about?"

He motioned for her to go first. "So who was this love who left you crushed and broken and in need of an immediate connection with someone else, as a way of recuperating?"

Taylor wanted to tell him. She couldn't. Not without sacrificing her pride and a whole lot else. She lined up her shot.

"What makes you think there was anyone who touched me that way?"

Jeremy grinned as her ball went left of the hole in the center of the cactus. "You wrote about being on the rebound with authenticity. To do that, on a soul-deep level, I'm guessing you would need to experience it."

"Or talk to a lot of people who have," Taylor countered lightly, making it on the second try.

Jeremy set his golf ball on the green. Hands on his club, he looked over at her, really curious now. For a quiet moment, he searched her face. "You're saying you got all your info by interviewing those who had loved and lost?"

Taylor watched with envy as he sank the ball in the target in one shot. Together, they sauntered toward the next hole, an overturned, oversized cowboy boot. "As a writer, you can imagine things and write about them based on the scenarios you dream up." Figuring he was due, she gave him a little grief. "For instance, you don't have to actually *experience* being in the middle of an avalanche to write about one. That's where research and creativity come in. That's why it's called *fiction*."

Her teasing tone made him smile. "Or in other words, you are not the heroine in your novel."

"Right." Taylor sank the second shot. "Although…" She straightened lazily, belatedly aware his eyes had been on her hips while she'd been taking her shot.

"What?"

She flushed, telling herself the sexual tension that had sprung up between them was natural—and easily discounted. Ignoring the slight catch in her breath, she explained, "There's a small part of me in every character I write. And a lot of people I meet and things I see are in my writing, too. Those little details are what give it authenticity. Writers observe, just like doctors. We pick up on little clues. Fit the pieces together."

Jeremy missed his second shot, as surely as she had missed her first. He picked up his ball and did it again, hitting his mark the second time. "Why did you and Baywatch Bart break up?"

If Taylor didn't know better, she would think this was vital information to him, instead of the kind of getting-to-know-each-other-better-chitchat friends exchanged when hanging out together.

She and Jeremy waited beneath an ivy-covered archway for the couple in front of them to finish on the third hole. Realizing she didn't mind him knowing the truth about this, even though it was something she rarely talked about, Taylor said, "Bart and I broke up because—like the characters in my novel—we both realized we were together for all the wrong reasons."

With Jeremy listening intently, Taylor continued, "When we met, we had both disappointed all those close to us by electing to make an unforeseen career change. Bart had almost finished law school but decided he didn't want to take the bar exam or join his father's law firm. He wanted to run a charter yacht service on the Atlantic seaboard. I had decided to drop out of medical school and pursue a career as a writer. Bart had been disinherited and disowned. I was similarly on the outs with my family back then. He had been summarily dumped by his fiancée. I—" She stopped abruptly, aware she had just said more than she'd intended.

"Go on," he urged.

Why shouldn't she say it? It wasn't as if Jeremy wouldn't understand. "I was interested in someone who was definitely not going to be interested in a struggling writer."

Jeremy scowled as the green cleared. Hand to her shoulder, he advanced with her into the next putting green, an over-turned stagecoach half buried in the "desert" sand.

Once again, Jeremy let her take the first shot. "Your 'crush' said that to you?"

"More or less." Embarrassed, Taylor focused on lining up golf ball and target. "Since my…um…crush didn't really know how I felt…the details don't matter. What is important is that when we first met, Bart and I both felt rejected, unsure of ourselves, in need of comfort, companionship and encouragement. So we hooked up—too fast—and started living together."

"Like the characters in your novel."

Taylor wet her suddenly parched lips with her tongue. "Right. That much I took from real life. But there was also a lot in that book, about the hero and the heroine, that had nothing to do with Bart or me."

Jeremy reached out to remove a strand of her hair from her cheek and tuck it behind her ear. Telling herself the thrill she felt was natural—she hadn't been touched with such man-woman reverence in forever—Taylor made an effort to pull herself together.

"Who did you base your characters on?"

"Everyone I've met who was in the same emotional place Bart and I were when we met." They both made their shots and progressed to the next green, where again they had to wait their turn.

"So what was the turning point?" Jeremy searched her eyes. "You were together for five years. How did you know it was over?"

Taylor shrugged. This was so much harder to put into words… "I think I knew by the time I finished my novel and sent it out to publishers that our relationship was over. I just didn't want to admit to myself that I had made the same mistake that my characters had. Bart realized it after the sale of my manuscript. By then his charter business was doing great, too. He knew how hard I had worked to become a published author. He was as happy and excited for me as I was for him and then he sat down to read the manuscript."

She took a deep breath. Jeremy squeezed her hand, encouraging her to continue.

Taylor had a far away expression on her face as she allowed the bittersweet memories to resurface. "He came out to tell me how much he liked the book. And I knew from the look on his face, that he realized that we were in a rebound relationship, too. We didn't feel the slightest inclination to marry each other and we both agreed he and I deserved more. So we split—amicably—like the characters in my novel."

"What did you do next?" Jeremy inquired gently.

"I started working on another book, in anticipation of the publication of my first, and then as soon as I had finished that, the first book came out. Zak and Zoe bought the rights to it, I was hired to write the screenplay—which I did—and then I had to go out to Los Angeles to be there for rewrites during the filming. And you know the rest…"

They progressed through the next series of holes, without delay. "When is your second book coming out?" Jeremy asked.

It was so easy to talk to him. "It's supposed to hit the stands around the same time as the movie and the reissue of my first book."

Jeremy sank another shot and turned to face her. "So what about this other guy—the crush who wasn't interested in a struggling writer. Is he interested in you now?"

Once again, Taylor put up an invisible force field around her. "It really doesn't matter. I've moved on."

He looked thoughtful.

"What about you?" Taylor forged on as they continued through the putt-putt course. "Did you have a rebound romance after you and Imogen broke up?"

"Imogen *was* my rebound. I was interested in someone before her who didn't see me that way."

He'd never said anything about an unrequited crush while they'd been in med school together, Taylor thought.

"I never put myself out there. I knew at the time it just wasn't going to work. So I looked for the first person who was sexy and exciting and hooked up with her instead. At the time I didn't think I was using Imogen. I thought we were giving each other the same level of commitment and attention."

"But she didn't think so."

"Imogen told me when she left me for that other guy that she knew I had never loved her. She thought the potential was there for both of us, but compared to what she had felt for the other guy, she knew we'd never had what it took."

"Amicably?"

He shrugged. "It was more like we wanted to move on and not look back. So we have. I think we were both embarrassed by our mistake and just wanted it to be over."

Taylor understood that all too well.

They finished the course, with a tie score, and headed to turn their equipment in. "Do you and Bart still talk?" Jeremy asked, stopping at the concession stand to buy them both a frozen cherry snow cone.

"Sometimes, yeah. But just as friends. He's married now. Expecting a baby." Treats in hand, they walked through the gates. Just in time for her soaring spirits to crash. "I can't believe it!" Taylor grimaced.

"What?"

Taylor gestured toward the black SUV pulling up at the curb. Zoe and Zak Townsend stepped out.

"YOU'RE A HARD WOMAN TO FIND," Zak said, coming toward them.

"Luckily," Zoe continued, "we ran into one of the camera men who was having dinner on Main Street tonight, and he said he saw you two walk out of the Jenna Lockhart boutique and head over here."

"Lucky us," Taylor muttered beneath her breath. "What did you need?"

"Let's talk in the SUV," Zoe said.

"Less chance of us being overheard," Zak agreed.

Taylor could not deny that the other people playing putt-putt were now a tad curious. "Fine. But Jeremy is coming with us. And so are our snow cones."

"We can get you snow cones, too, if you like," Jeremy offered.

"All that sugar?" Zak sneered.

"And artificial flavoring?" Zoe added. "Please!"

Zak opened the side door in the specially outfitted vehicle. Their driver/bodyguard climbed out. The second and third seat were facing each other, the same as if they would be in a limo. Zak and Zoe sat beside each other in the second seat. Taylor and Jeremy took the third.

"So what's up?" Taylor asked.

"We've found a location. We're going to start filming that first desert scene at seven tomorrow morning." Zak handed over a map and instructions on how to get there. "We've got *Access L.A.* and Celebrity Entertainment Network crews coming to do coverage on the unfortunate rumors surrounding the three of us."

Taylor tensed. This is where she drew the line. "I have nothing to say to them."

"Actually, you do," Zak corrected firmly while tightly holding his wife's hand.

"We need you to be there and act strictly professional in your interactions with both of us. And if you can bring someone else along—" Zoe waved at Jeremy "—like your friend here—"

Jeremy supplied his name dryly. "Jeremy."

"Right," Zoe continued with a nod of acknowledgement. "If you could bring Jeremy to make out with behind the scenes—obviously you'll need to make it look like you're trying *not* to get caught—"

"When really we are," Taylor guessed.

Zak leered at Taylor "That would go a long way toward dispelling these ugly rumors about the two of us."

Jeremy looked ready to deck Zak.

"Because naturally," Zoe interrupted, "we all know they aren't true. The tabloids are just doctoring photos and making up stories to sell papers. And rather than investigate it properly, the legitimate news sources are starting to run with it."

Jeremy exhaled, his patience fading as fast as Taylor's. "Well, then, why not just go on record and say it's not true?" he asked.

"Because Taylor is not used to being on camera and her nervousness could make it look like she is lying," Zak said.

Taylor polished off her snow cone. "I don't want to be interviewed about this. I'd prefer to just let all the ugly innuendo fade away naturally, over time. To speed that process along, I think it would be better if I had no personal interaction with either of you from now on, period. If there is nothing going on, there will be nothing to report."

"That won't work." Zoe disagreed with a definitive shake of her head. "We've already promised the *Access L.A.* and Celebrity Entertainment Network crews they'll be able to get glimpses of you, working the set, as well as in-depth interviews with us. The cameras will be rolling seven o'clock tomorrow morning. Be there. And Taylor, don't wear makeup or do your hair. Try to look as unattractive as possible. That way people will be even more sure that nothing is going on between you and Zak."

Taylor wasn't sure how she did it, but somehow she maintained her deadpan expression. "Good tip." Taylor got out of the SUV and Jeremy followed. The driver climbed back in and drove off.

Jeremy stared after them with disgust. "Those two take total self-absorbedness to new heights."

Taylor tossed their empty paper cones in the trash can and let out a beleaguered sigh. "Ignore what those two idiots just said. You don't have to go."

"I wouldn't miss it for the world," Jeremy insisted. "Now, how about some pizza?"

JEREMY WAS WAITING FOR HER when she emerged from the bedroom at six-thirty the next morning. He was dressed in a stylish ecru T-shirt, jeans and boots. He had a straw cowboy hat in his hand. He looked pure Texas and handsome enough to fall in love with. Not that she was planning to fall in love with him, she amended hastily. The two of them had already proved they were too different to get romantically involved.

Jeremy gazed appreciatively at her long cocoa-colored skirt, white embroidered lace sleeveless V-neck top and high-heeled western boots. As always, she'd donned her gold shamrock necklace, for luck, and spent extra time on her upswept hair and makeup. The spritz of perfume she had added to her throat, behind her ears, and her cleavage had been just for the hell of it.

Jeremy grinned, clearly approving of the time she had spent getting ready. "Not so good at following orders, are you?" he teased.

Taylor didn't even try to suppress a chuckle. "I'm hoping if I look too good Zoe will get jealous, have me make the promised appearance, and then send me home early."

"Smart." He nodded, settling his hat on his head.

"You ready to go?" she asked.

"You bet." He fell into step right behind her. "Ready to make out with you, too—as ordered."

Feeling his gaze skimming the backside of her every bit as carefully as he had just perused her front, she slowed her pace, so they were walking side by side. She gave him a reproving glance. "Just so you know… We're not *really* going to do that."

"I don't know." Jeremy rubbed his jaw in a parody of thoughtfulness. "If duty calls…"

Taylor flushed at the memory of his lips on hers, and the fervent wish, that it would happen again someday. "Trust me." She paused next to the passenger side of his pickup truck and tapped the rock-solid center of his chest. "I'll be there because my showing up on demand is in my contract with their production company, and I want to get this over and done with and get paid, but beyond that… They are not telling me who to kiss and when and where! And if they think they can, they've got another think coming!"

"Hold on there, 'Nellie'." Jeremy clamped both his hands on her slender shoulders. His touch was warm and evocative. "No sense in getting riled up before you have to be."

Taylor looked into his eyes, surprised at the comfort—and the banked desire—she found there. "You're right."

"I'm sure Zoe and Zak will give you plenty of opportunity to get ticked off once we get there."

How right Jeremy was about that, Taylor thought, an hour later.

No sooner had they arrived at the set, than one of Zoe's many assistants called Taylor and Jeremy to the silver Gulfstream trailer, which served as Zoe's dressing room. It was filled with fresh flowers, as well as photos and posters of Zoe.

Zoe, who had been having the final touches put on her hair, shooed her entourage out of the trailer. She was dressed in native Indian garb. She had lace-up faux leather moccasins on her feet and a feather headdress in her hair. "We made some changes to those pages you wrote," she said.

"Of course." Taylor had ceased to be surprised by anything Zak or Zoe did.

"First of all, we like the fact that it's going to be a dream sequence. But we don't think Zak should be unfaithful in his fantasies, so I am going to be the Indian woman who comes to him and imparts the crucial wisdom."

"O-kay." At this point, Taylor could really care less. She just wanted it over. It didn't matter that the revised pages she had ended up writing would have imparted new depth to the characters. It was all too clear from this ridiculous Indian get-up that they'd missed the whole concept, and all her hard work had once again been hideously revised by Zak and Zoe. She had known when commissioned to do the extra work that only a tenth of what she actually worked on would actually make it into the movie. Right now, she was hoping the finished film would go straight to video and be promptly forgotten. Even if it went to the theaters as is—which she doubted—it wouldn't stay there long. People would not pay to see that mess.

"The *Access L.A.* and the Celebrity Entertainment Network crews are already here. So you two can say hello, then do your best to avoid them, and just go somewhere and try to get caught making out—the hotter the heavier the better. Zak and I are going to do the same. Okay?"

"Got it." Taylor smiled and eased out of the trailer, before she could be told to do anything even more ludicrous.

Jeremy whispered in her ear, "You know, I wouldn't believe this if I hadn't just—Hi." He smiled at the camera crew suddenly in his face.

"Taylor…Jeremy, it's reported in the *New York Daily Express* today that you two are getting married, and that Jenna Lockhart Designs will be supplying the wedding gown and tuxedo. Any comment?"

Taylor opened her mouth, then promptly shut it, looked at Jeremy. He was as at a loss as she was. "No," Jeremy said, putting his arm around Taylor's waist. "I don't think we do. But Zoe might have something to say. Why don't you go on in?" Ever the gallant Texan, he opened the door to the trailer.

Delighted, the camera crew entered.

As soon as they had passed, Jeremy grabbed Taylor's hand. "Quick."

Too late, the CEN crew had already caught up with them.

"Taylor. We're doing a piece for the CEN show, *Short-takes!* Are you having an affair with Zak Townsend?"

"No. Absolutely not," Taylor said.

"Then can you tell us about those reports of you kissing him before you left California?"

"It's not true," Taylor said simply, looking in the camera. "Beyond that, I have nothing to say." She held up a hand in front of her face. Jeremy wrapped an arm about her waist and helped her push past them.

"Zoe, on the other hand, has plenty to say," Jeremy said over his shoulder, "and she's in there." He pointed to the trailer.

While the CEN crew tried to gain entrance to Zoe's lair, Jeremy and Taylor headed for the shade of the makeup trailer, located on the edge of the set. "Is this where we make out?" Jeremy asked.

"Very funny."

Taylor peered around the corner and glimpsed the camera crew coming out of Zoe's trailer. Moments later the stars emerged and one of the assistants told Zoe and Zak they were about ready to start filming.

"We should have a reprieve." Taylor ducked back into the shade, out of sight.

"Don't you want to watch the filming?" Jeremy asked.

"Please. It's painful enough, just knowing they've already

changed most of the words they demanded I write. I can only take so much punishment."

"Is that what you call this?"

Taylor leaned against the side of the trailer and tried not to feel too ill about everything that had happened. "Unless you are the kind of writer who can sell a work, let it go emotionally and not look back, you should never sell your story to the movie industry. For me, each book is like a baby that I've carried close to my heart, nurtured and brought to life. There's no amount of money—or fame—that is ever going to be worth the way they've butchered my story to make this movie. But…live and learn, I guess."

Compassion underscored his low tone. "Maybe it's not as bad as you think."

Taylor took Jeremy by the arm and took him around the other way, so they could stand, unobserved, while Zak and Zoe attempted to act out a dream sequence. "Okay," Jeremy said after a moment, sorrowfully shaking his head, "maybe it is that bad." He guided her back to the shade, so they were in seclusion once again. "The thing you have to remember is that it will be over soon."

One could hope. Taylor tipped her head back against the side of the trailer and looked up at him. "Promise?" she said.

JEREMY hadn't planned on kissing Taylor. At least not here, when they'd been "directed" to do so. The way she was looking at him changed that.

He saw the hurt and disappointment in her eyes, the regret. The story she had worked so long and hard on was being systematically destroyed by two selfish fame junkies. And there wasn't a damn thing either of them could do about it.

However, there *was* something he could do about the mounting cynicism she was trying so hard to hide. He could show her there was still much in this world that was pure and good, that there were other ways—besides their work—they could find true, soul-deep satisfaction.

And it was right here and right now. Between the two of them. Just waiting to be had. All he had to do was…

"Jeremy." Reading his intention, she splayed both her hands across his chest.

He felt her tremble, even as her lips parted. "I know." He sifted his fingers through her hair, cupped her face in his hands. "It's a bad idea." His lips touched hers, however briefly. "Wrong place." He kissed her again, lightly. "Wrong time."

Her eyes closed. "Wrong…everything," she whispered back.

He let himself revel in the taste and feel of her, so soft and womanly. "Only thing is," he whispered back, between tender kisses, "it doesn't feel wrong." Sliding one hand down her back, he brought her closer yet. "It feels…right."

She turned her head. He explored the delicate outer shell of her ear, the graceful nape of her neck, the U of her collarbone. And heard her moan.

She turned her lips back to his. "I knew seeing you again was going to be trouble," she said.

He chuckled loving the sound of her voice, the feel of her body as she rose up on tiptoe, pressing her warm yielding body against his. That small sign of surrender was all it took. His gentlemanly restraint fled. Hands on her shoulders, he trapped her between the trailer and his body. Their bodies grew closer, their kiss intensified, until she was all he felt, all he knew, all he wanted. It was then, when the fire between them had the potential to burn so much hotter that they heard a clank, an oath, and felt a bright light shining down upon them.

They broke apart, muttering their mutual dismay. And found themselves staring, wide-eyed, into yet another camera.

Chapter Eight

"And now for the latest on the scandal surrounding the Zak and Zoe movie." Host Jonathon Moore looked into the camera and flashed a teasing smile.

"Is the sexy novelist now torn between two lovers? Our recent visit to the set of *Sail Away* showed us that the gossip surrounding scribe Taylor O'Quinn and handsome local hunk, Dr. Jeremy Carrigan, is all true. The couple were spotted making out behind the craft trailer during filming. As you can see, Taylor and Jeremy weren't all that thrilled when the camera crew and I stumbled upon them.

(Cut to blurry footage of the two lovebirds rushing past, hands held in front of their faces, muttering "No Comment!" to the questions being fired at them.)

"Zak and Zoe Townsend seemed equally into each other."

(More footage, this time of Zak and Zoe making out, hot and heavy, just outside the door of Zoe's trailer.)

"But the photos taken two days before, show a different story."

(Still photos showed Zak on the dance floor, an intent look on his face, Taylor O'Quinn in his arms.)

"And still more developments," Jonathon continued salaciously, "one day ago."

(Another photo of Taylor, trying on wedding dresses at the prestigious Jenna Lockhart boutique, while Jeremy Carrigan sat on the sofa, watching with an admiring grin.)

"One beau is already married. The other seems to be offering marriage. Which one will Taylor choose? Stay tuned…"

Access L.A. syndicated television show
June 8.

Jeremy waited until they were well on the way home before he spoke. He turned his glance away from the wheel of his pickup truck long enough to ask, "Are you ever going to speak to me again?"

Taylor folded her arms in front of her. The action served to emphasize the soft curves of her breasts beneath the lacy tank top.

Her lips set in a feisty pout, she stared straight ahead. "You should be glad I'm *not* engaging you in dialogue right now!"

Jeremy knew Taylor'd had a hell of a day. Her hope of being dismissed early had not been granted. Instead, she had been forced to stand around, cooling her heels, smiling and interacting professionally with Zoe, Zak, and the film's director—all for benefit of the showbiz reporters and film crews.

It had been hard enough for Jeremy, after they'd been caught making out behind the trailer. It was worse for Taylor. For starters, Zak and Zoe had changed nearly every line Taylor had written—most of which, Jeremy thought had been damn good—into trendy gibberish.

He didn't think the constant tinkering with the material was malicious. Zak and Zoe just did not know what the heck they were doing. They weren't actors…they weren't writers. They did have an acute sense of presentation, however. And they knew when they were out of their depth. Both were trying desperately not to make fools of themselves with the first project their production company, Always Famous, helmed.

Unfortunately, the more they tried, the more they failed. And everyone on the set—from the cast and crew to the makeup artists and hairstylists—knew it.

Pink color sweeping into her cheeks, Taylor continued her tirade. "I told you I did not want to make out with you just because I was told to!"

Willing to be the temporary target of her angst if it made her feel better, Jeremy said, "I didn't want you to do that, either."

She tossed her head. Strands of silky black hair, already tousled from the wind, swished softly about her shoulders. "But you did want to make out with me!"

Jeremy shrugged. "I'm not going to deny I enjoyed it," he told her frankly, glad they were nearly at their destination, so he'd be able to stop driving and focus all his attention on her. "And if you were honest, you'd admit you enjoyed it, too."

"That's not the point." Arms still folded militantly in front of her, Taylor settled deeper into her half of the bench-style front seat. "The point is it was embarrassing, Jeremy!"

More than that, Jeremy thought ruefully. The interruption had ruined the moment, turned what could have been a turning point in their relationship into a fiasco.

Struggling to contain his own emotions, he turned on his right signal light. "I'm disappointed about the intrusion, too. The difference is, I am determined not to let it ruin the rest of my day."

Taylor's eyes widened at the direction his truck took. "Where are you going?" she demanded. "The Chamberlain ranch is down that road."

"My ranch is this way."

She released an indignant breath and looked so pretty all he could think about was kissing her again. "I need to stop by there. It will just take a minute."

"I'm really not in the mood for this, Jeremy," she told him.

There was no way he was going to let them part when she was still this upset about the way the Townsends had used her and defamed her reputation to further their own skyrocketing careers.

Jeremy turned into the entrance of Lago Vista Ranch. He hoped—if nothing else—the changes he had made would serve as a distraction. Taylor's scowl faded as they passed the thicket of trees near the entrance and came upon what was now a newly shorn meadow. She looked at the manicured grass with obvious pleasure. "Who did this?"

Jeremy felt an unaccustomed burst of pride. In the past, his accomplishments had been pretty much limited to his work. "I did it yesterday." He slowed the truck to a crawl. It bumped over the rough gravel lane. He was going to have to get this paved…

"My brother-in-law, Tyler, lent me the tractor with mowing attachment that he uses at his ranch." It had been immensely satisfying to turn an overgrown mess into a property that was beautiful, private and filled with the rugged character of the West Texas countryside.

Taylor noted the ripe fruit glistening against green leaves. "You left the blackberry bushes!"

Obviously, a good move on his part. "I saw you eyeing them the other day."

"I'm still eying them." Taylor grabbed his arm, her delicate fingers curling around his bicep. Warmth flowed through him. "Let's stop and pick some now!"

"Right now?" In the heat of the late afternoon? When she was dressed that nicely?

"Yes! It's been years since I've had fresh-picked blackberries. If we get enough we could take them back to the Chamberlain ranch and make cobbler or jam."

Jeremy did a U-turn and drove his truck to the edge of the thicket. He cut the engine and vaulted from the cab at the same time as she. They met in front. She beamed like a kid about to open presents on Christmas Day.

He reached behind the seat and took out a stack of brown paper lunch sacks he'd started carrying after the Krista Sue hyperventilation incident for house calls and other emergencies.

Taylor lifted a berry to her lips. A sinful expression came over her face. "I know you're supposed to wash these first…"

He watched her savor the sweet, juicy fruit. "Too delicious to resist?"

"Something like that." Grinning, she popped a few more into her mouth, instead of the bag.

"Well?" He came close enough to wipe a drop of juice from the center of her lower lip. "Did it live up to your expectation?"

"Try one and tell me what you think," she said instead, putting one against his lips. The sensation of her fingers against his lip sent desire roaring through him.

She waited.

"Nothing like ripe berry," he said.

"Except maybe one thing."

"That being?" She turned to him with a curious smile.

"Guess."

THIS TIME, Taylor saw the kiss coming. Knew she could have resisted. Probably should have. But something about the sun and the taste of ripe berry still in her mouth and on his lips drove her to forget being cautious and just go with the moment.

He was strong…he was gentle. His kisses were incredibly

sexy and evocative. He was also, unfortunately, a pillar of re-straint, ending the steamy embrace all too soon.

He looked down at her. "We better keep going," he said, after a moment, with a grin that promised her this was not the last time they'd end up together. A look that said, like fine wine, the ardor between them would only get better with time.

He traced the curve of her cheek with the backs of his fingers. "Or we'll likely be here all night, trying to get enough berries to do everything you want to do with them."

"True." Heart pounding, Taylor went back to picking berries. Her lips continued to tingle. Lower still, she felt a flut-tering in her tummy she couldn't deny.

Drawing on every ounce of self-restraint she had, she went back to picking berries. While they filled their paper lunch sacks to overflowing, and started on two others, she asked Jeremy about his life in Laramie. "Do you ever feel hemmed in? Coming back to work where you grew up?"

He shook his head. "I was away for nine years, if you count college, med school, internship and residency. That was long enough to realize where I wanted to be, which is right here. I love the people, the wide open spaces, the climate. The only downside is that since I grew up here, a lot of people remember me as a kid. They have a hard time accepting me as a physician. It's like, in theory they trust me to take care of their health, but in reality can't quite do it, not without checking up on me and anything I prescribe first."

"So there's a lot of Internet research going on, I gather." Her skirt snagged on a branch.

Jeremy came over to help disentangle her. "That and turn-ing to doctors like my dad who've been here forever for second opinions just to be sure I know what I am doing."

"That must suck," Taylor said sympathetically.

"Yeah. It does. But I'm told over time the lack of trust in me will be replaced by unshakable faith in my abilities."

"Well, I'm sure that day couldn't come quickly enough for you," she said with a smile.

"Speaking of future things," Jeremy drawled cheerfully as he took their full sacks of berries and carried them over to his truck. "Since I finally got the message I needed to get my act together to make my dream ranch a reality, don't you think we ought to go and see what progress has been made today in my absence?"

THE CLOSER JEREMY GOT to the actual ranch house, the tenser he got. He wasn't afraid he was going to be disappointed. Heck, anything would be an improvement over what the conditions had been. He was worried what had been done thus far wouldn't live up to Taylor's standards. And how crazy was that? It wasn't as if he needed her approval. Or that any of this should matter to her. She wasn't going to live here. She wasn't going to even be in Laramie that much longer. Still, he wanted to impress her with his efforts. Which made him feel all of say...sixteen.

"Well. I don't see anyone," Taylor remarked as Jeremy parked in front of the ranch house.

However, they could see where the dirt had been moved, fresh sod laid down, a short distance from the oddly shaped ranch house. "They must have finished putting in the new septic tank," Jeremy said.

"Is that the central air-conditioning unit?" Taylor pointed to the large metal box with the wire grate on top, located just next to the ranch house.

Jeremy nodded. "They must be done, too. Otherwise they would still be here."

"You didn't have to pay them before they left?"

Jeremy shook his head, aware Laramie businesses operated on a level of trust not generally found in the big cities. "I did that up front. Told them to leave the key under the mat when they were done, the instructions next to the thermostat."

"Now I'm curious. Let's go see!" Taylor leaped out of the truck before he could swing around to help her with her door.

Determined to play it cool, Jeremy took his time catching up. Yet there was no downplaying the lift in his spirits when he swung open the front door and was confronted with a blast of cool air.

"Wow!" Taylor moved past the front rooms where the walls had been knocked out, the debris cleared, and into the family room and stopped abruptly. "You've got..."

"Attic hand-me-downs." An odd assortment of furniture sat in the center of the room. She turned in delight, question in her eyes. "My family took pity on me." Jeremy continued, clapping a hand to the back of his neck as he studied his old furniture, some of which had definitely seen better days. "That and I think they wanted to get rid of all this stuff," he said dryly, knowing a few slipcovers and a little refinishing here and there would work wonders.

The surprise was he *wanted* to work wonders.

He had never cared much about interior furnishings before. Or anything to do with décor. If he could sit on a chair, he was satisfied. Now, well, he could see it might not hurt to actually be *comfortable*.

"This is great!" Taylor glided forward to inspect his cache. "You've got an easy chair and a sofa. A reading lamp and side table. Even a coffee table to put your feet up on! And a fridge in the kitchen!"

Jeremy turned to follow her glance. Taylor appeared as excited about the pint-sized dorm fridge he'd installed— temporarily—as she would have been over a large sub-zero unit. "And a hot plate and toaster oven. Not to mention a folding table to put them on!"

He grinned, liking her style. Most women would have looked at all this and complained…bitterly. At the very least, made endless fun of him. Hands in his pockets, he hovered closer. "You get excited about the silliest things."

She didn't think so. Turning, she clapped her hands together and declared, "Now all you need is a bed."

"That," he interrupted, "I've got. I called the furniture store yesterday and had them deliver one. I figured if I had central air and heat and plumbing I had no excuse not to be living out here."

Briefly, disappointment shadowed her eyes. "So you'll be leaving the Chamberlain ranch," she said, as if it were no big deal.

"As soon as I get my stuff out, yeah." Suddenly, Jeremy felt disappointed about that, too. Primarily because it meant he would no longer be seeing her morning, noon and night.

Taylor recovered. "Of course you will." She shook her head sheepishly, and ran her hands through her hair. "I don't know what I was thinking." She stepped away from him and continued looking around.

Jeremy followed at leisure. "Maybe that I was too chicken to ever live here?" he teased softly.

She whirled so suddenly she nearly bumped into his chest. "Hey, I didn't say that."

"But you thought it," he guessed.

She collected herself and moved back slightly. "Last week, maybe, but not any more." She paused to look into his eyes. "You're on your way to having your coveted ranch a home, Jeremy, at long last."

He ought to be happy about that, but all he could think was he wouldn't be seeing Taylor every morning. And every night. Feelings in turmoil—he wasn't used to his happiness depending on the presence of anyone else—he walked into the wing that held the master bedroom.

There it was, in the center of the room. A mattress and box spring on a plain metal frame, already made up with plain white cotton sheets, a blanket and two pillows. Several boxes stood on the floor in the corner. They were heaped with an odd assortment of towels, washcloths, a white vinyl shower curtain, and additional bed linens that once again did not begin to match up, never mind go with the room. A note perched atop it said,

Jeremy,
No more excuses on why you can't stay here…!
P.S.—When you decide on a permanent color scheme, we've decided to chip in and get you real linens for this room. In the meantime, these should do…
Love, Susie, Amy and Rebecca

"That was nice of your sisters," Taylor murmured, reading the note, too.

No, it wasn't, Jeremy thought. They were giving him no excuse to go back to the Chamberlain ranch tonight. Except to drop Taylor off. Without that proximity, with him having to go to work at the hospital tomorrow morning, how was he supposed to get close to Taylor again in record time?

Scowling, he went to the tap and turned it on. He watched the water go down the drain and continue to run perfectly. He tried the shower. Same thing. And the toilet actually flushed.

Taylor was right beside him. "Everything seems to be working," she said.

"Hallelujah," Jeremy muttered.

Taylor studied him, taking in his surly tone. A slow smile curved her lips and crinkled the corners of her eyes. "I think I know what the problem is," she said eventually.

Jeremy scoffed, not used to having a woman read his

mind—with any success anyway. "You can't possibly know what I'm thinking."

"Sure I do." Taylor regarded him playfully. "You're scared to spend the night out here alone and frankly, I don't blame you! First night in a new place? Out here in the boonies?" She tapped the center of his chest with her index finger. "I'd be spooked, too."

Jeremy captured her hand and held it against his sternum. "I'm not spooked."

"Then stay out here tonight," she dared.

"Only," Jeremy proposed right back, drawing her even closer, "if you stay with me."

"NOW WAIT JUST A MINUTE," Taylor said as Jeremy wrapped both his arms around her and brought them into full frontal contact. "How did this become *my* problem?"

"Because you made it your problem?" he murmured, his lips tracing a fiery path from her temple to her lips.

Feeling the heat of his arousal, sensations swept through Taylor. "You've only got one bed," she protested weakly.

His hands roamed up and down her spine. "Ah, but I've got a sofa."

She moaned. "Is that really why you want me here?" she queried softly, trying to figure out what this all meant. Were they friends? Or something more? Something…lasting?

"Are you trying to prove a point?" Say that he was a gentleman rancher after all, not just a wannabe.

"The only thing I want to prove," he said huskily, folding her even closer, "is this."

The next thing she knew, his lips were on hers, making way for the hot thrust of his tongue, and she was too caught up in the moment to think rationally. She knew taking their relationship to the next level was risky but he tasted and felt so good, so undeniably male. It had been a long time since she had felt so beautiful and so wanted. Desire trembled inside her, and she reveled in the thrill of his deep, mesmerizing kisses. She wanted to feel connected to him, not just physically, but emotionally, too.

Looking more determined than she'd ever seen him, he took her by the hand and guided her over to the bed. Taylor tangled her fingers in his hair and caught his head between her hands. A melting warmth raced through her as they began to kiss once again. His hands went from her back to her breasts, slipping beneath her tank top, and bra, circling the aching crowns and teasing her nipples into tight buds of aching desire. Overwhelmed by the hot, masculine taste of him, she kissed the corners of his mouth, probed his mouth with her tongue, then let him kiss her more deeply. Bit by bit, her inhibitions slipped away, and still they kissed, until her heartbeat hammered in her ears and she could hardly catch her breath.

"I want you," Jeremy whispered against her throat.

Quivering with sensations unlike any she had ever felt, Taylor's hand went to the zipper on her skirt. "I want you, too."

He caught her hand. "Let me."

She throbbed with excitement as he eased the tank top over her head, the skirt down her hips. Clad only in two pieces of ecru lace, she reached for the buttons on his shirt. "You, too."

His smile widened seductively as that came off, along with his boots and jeans.

Their breath rasped as the rest of their clothing came off, too. He caught her hand and drew her down onto the sheets.

She looked her fill.

He looked his.

"Beautiful," he murmured.

"You are, too."

And so was this moment, Taylor thought, as the sheer

physical abandon she had always wanted to feel took over. It felt so right to have him stretched out beside her. New sensations blossomed.

The inviting look in Taylor's eyes, the soft yielding of her kiss and touch, was all the encouragement Jeremy needed to make Taylor his woman, once and for all. Aware they had waited far too long as it was, he wedged a knee between her thighs and kissed her again. She kissed him back, and he flattened one hand beneath her, using the other to touch her dewy softness, to possess, to stroke. His own body throbbing, he loved her, discovered her, until she was arching up off the bed, urging him to completion.

Unable to get enough of her, he plunged inside her silky heat. Her head fell back, her body shuddered, and then she was trembling all over, inside and out, stunning him with the sheer sensuality of her response. Passion flooded through Jeremy in fiery, all-encompassing waves. Never passive, she took the lead and went right on kissing him, slow and easy, hard and fast, until their bodies took up a primitive rhythm all their own. She opened herself up to him, surrendering the depths of her womanhood, the very essence of her heart and soul. Knowing they were one, feeling closer to her than he ever had before, he made love to her fiercely. And then, awash in pleasure, all was lost in the sweeping ascent to ecstasy, and the softer, slower fall back.

Chapter Nine

Broke, Desperate, and…Pregnant?

Recent photos (see below) suggest all is not well with
Zak Townsend's "alleged" mistress, Taylor O'Quinn.
First, Ms. Quinn was forced to leave her Hollywood
Love Nest—aka rundown studio apartment—(see
photo 1)—for rural Texas. Down to her last penny, she
is reduced to foraging for berries (photo 2) with backup
lover, Dr. Jeremy Carrigan. Does her thickening waist-
line (photo 3) indicate a baby is on the way?
And if so, whose child is it?

TRASHTALK.com
June 9

"Okay, what's going on?" Paige drawled, walking into the
Chamberlain ranch house kitchen. "I leave for the weekend
and you two are barely speaking. I come back and now you're
all cozy."

It was a remarkable turn of events, Taylor acknowledged.
One she hadn't seen coming.

Jeremy looked at Taylor, the fire of their lovemaking, just

hours earlier, still in his eyes. "We came to an understanding," he explained.

And then some, Taylor thought, aware she had never been happier.

"Uh-huh. And now you're cooking dinner together?" Paige eyed the sizzling steak platter on the center of the table. An open bottle of red wine sat next to it.

Smug male confidence radiated from Jeremy. "Man's gotta eat."

Unable to help but think how cozy and intimate it felt to be there with Jeremy like this, Taylor said, "Woman, too."

Despite their careless banter, Paige did not look fooled. Her friend knew intuitively, Taylor thought, that this was so much more than a passing fling for Taylor. Otherwise, Taylor would not have tumbled into bed with Jeremy. The question was, how did Jeremy feel, deep inside? Did he just enjoy being with her? Or was he too now looking for something more? His handsome face gave no clue to what was in his heart. And certainly it was way too soon for either of them to be talking about even the possibility of falling in love, never mind living happily ever after….

Oblivious to Taylor's line of thinking, Jeremy got out a third place setting. "Join us," he urged Paige.

"Love to." Paige surveyed the trays of blackberries Taylor and Jeremy had washed and left on the countertop to dry.

Taylor took the blackberry cobbler out of the oven. "How was the wedding?"

"Depressing." Paige grimaced and sipped her wine. "Not for them. They were very happy. For me. Seeing them, seeing the two of you, seeing practically everyone else in the world paired up, just reminds me I don't have a special someone in my life."

"First of all," Taylor flushed, "Jeremy and I aren't paired up."

"Could have fooled me," Paige scoffed.

"Me, too," Jeremy said.

Paige's brow rose at the possessive note in Jeremy's voice. Taylor avoided Jeremy's eyes. *So much for his ability to be discreet.* "When it comes to matters of the heart, I have always favored a conservative approach," she said stiffly. As much as she might not want to think it, just because she and Jeremy had made love did not mean theirs was a lasting connection. Permanent relationships took a lot of time, commitment, shared values, hopes and dreams. She didn't even know what Jeremy's dreams were—other than being a doctor and a gentleman rancher.

"And where has the cautious approach gotten you?" Paige asked Taylor. "Or you?" She looked at Jeremy. "Or me for that matter? Nowhere! I tell you, this weekend I realized I am not getting any younger. Time's flying. And if I don't start making some changes, I might end up growing old alone."

"If this is what it's going to do to you, maybe you shouldn't go to any more weddings," Jeremy suggested.

Paige waved off his wry advice. "How did the additional filming for *Sail Away* go?"

Taylor and Jeremy groaned in unison. He mimed putting his hands around his head like a vice. "I had no idea Zak and Zoe were so…"

"Stupid…shallow…self-absorbed?" Taylor filled in the blank for him.

"And then some." Jeremy shook his head in disgust, then went on, perplexed, "I mean, like the rest of America, I saw bits and pieces of their reality TV show, and even clips of their concert act. I thought the silly self-conceit was all for show, that they couldn't be that unaware and had to be playing it for laughs."

"Instead, it's all careful editing?" Paige guessed.

Taylor's cell phone began to ring.

"Are you going to answer that?" Jeremy asked.

"I don't even want to look at my messages until morning. Because if I look at it and it's Zak or Zoe again—or one of their entourage—I'm just going to scream."

"Then I'll look," Paige, a fervent believer in always checking your messages, said. "Uh-oh."

Taylor tensed. "What?"

Paige made a face. "It's your parents."

THE LAST TIME Jeremy had seen Taylor look so distressed was the day she'd told her family she was dropping out of medical school.

"Mom, Dad!" Taylor rushed out into the driveway the moment her parents drove up.

Curtailing the increasing protectiveness he felt toward her, he too went to greet their unexpected guests.

Flushing bright pink, Taylor hugged them both. "You should have let me know you were coming!"

"We tried," Taylor's mother, a handsome woman in her midfifties, said.

Her dad added in exasperation, "We've been calling you since two o'clock this afternoon." He ran his hand through his salt-and-pepper hair. "Don't you ever look at your messages?"

"I was out on location," Taylor explained, lifting both palms in the age-old gesture of surrender. "There's no cell phone coverage out there."

Her parents looked past Taylor. "Paige…Jeremy. How great to see you both!" The women hugged. The men shook hands. "We hear both your medical practices are going great," Taylor's dad said.

"We couldn't be prouder of you two," her mother added.

Jeremy wasn't surprised to hear that. Norah and Phil O'Quinn were both on the faculty of the medical school in Dallas that the three of them had attended. Devoted teachers as well as incredibly talented physicians, Norah and Phil kept up with all their former students and beamed over their success.

They had also never gotten over the fact their only daughter had dropped out, before realizing the dream they'd had for her. It didn't matter they'd had two sons—Clint and Adam—who had followed in their footsteps. They'd wanted Taylor to be a part of their profession, too.

"You're welcome to stay the night," Paige said, gesturing toward the ranch house. "We've got plenty of guest rooms."

"Thanks but we're on our way to Big Bend for a medical conference slash vacation. We just stopped by to speak to Taylor."

It was obvious Phil and Norah O'Quinn did not want an audience for what they were about to say, Jeremy thought.

"All right, then, I'll leave you to it." Paige smiled, then turned and aimed a level look in his direction. "Jeremy, I could use a hand with those dishes."

Taylor looked at Jeremy like she also wanted him to go.

"Right." Reluctantly, he followed Paige into the ranch house.

"Would you like to sit down?" Taylor gestured toward the chairs around the swimming pool. "I'm guessing from the looks on your faces, you've heard something about the controversy."

Norah sniffed in distress. "It would be hard not to know about your alleged love affairs with Zak Townsend and Jeremy Carrigan."

"It's all over the airwaves, the Internet, on the cover of every supermarket tabloid," Phil added.

"Yes, well," Taylor sighed, "I'm trying not to look at any of that."

Phil's eyes narrowed. "You can't ignore this."

Taylor did not know about that. "I seem to be doing a pretty good job so far."

Her mother leaned forward urgently. "Honey, we know

these things aren't true. They're just stories made up to sell papers and magazines."

Taylor's shoulders relaxed slightly. "Thank you for that."

"We know Jeremy," her father continued. "He would never take advantage of you. And you're too smart to let some pop-rock star seduce you into breaking up his marriage."

Taylor studied her folks. "If you know that…then why the concern?"

"We want to help you hire a publicist to manage all this bad press," her mother said.

Taylor blinked in surprise. "That's really kind of you, but…no."

"Be reasonable, Taylor," her father pressed.

Taylor rose and began to pace. "I'm not going to dignify these stories with a publicity blitz of my own. They'll die down on their own. They always do after a couple of weeks," she soothed. "The movie is almost finished—we've only got one more day of filming and that is tomorrow, at the soundstage—and then Zak and Zoe Townsend will be out of my life."

Her parents studied her, finally asking, "What about the movie premiere? You're going to attend that, aren't you?"

Taylor shook her head. "At this point, probably not. In fact the more I can distance myself from this film, the better."

"What about Jeremy?" her mother probed.

Taylor didn't follow. "What about him?"

Her father stood, too. "You chose this career. And with your sale of your novel to the movies, you also selected this very public Hollywood life. Jeremy didn't, Taylor. You need to consider that."

"In what sense?" Taylor stared at her parents, confused.

Her mother explained gently, "The public expects people associated with the entertainment industry to be a little flaky and get caught up in all the ridiculous trappings of celebrity. They hold their *family physicians* to a different standard. The people we know in Dallas are all talking about this."

Taylor backed away from them both. "It's different in Laramie. The people are not impressed by celebrities, and they don't care about their private lives and misfortunes."

"Maybe not yet," her father warned.

"But they will," her mother predicted.

Her father agreed. "We don't know what has been going on between you and Jeremy, but we do know it's not good for his career and professional reputation." Phil paused to give weight to his words. "If you care about him at all, you'll leave him out of this, Taylor. You'll walk away."

"HOW'S IT GOING OUT THERE?" Paige asked.

Jeremy wished they hadn't finished the dishes so quickly. He could have used something to do. "Doesn't look good— for Taylor anyway."

Paige shook her head in distress. "Man, I feel for her."

From where he was standing, Jeremy could see the anxious expression on Taylor's face. "Me, too."

Paige turned away from the windows overlooking the pool. "My parents have always supported me, no matter what I chose to do."

Jeremy exhaled. "Mine, too."

Paige picked up her keys, purse and weekend travel bag she'd dumped next to the back door. "You'll make sure she's okay?"

Jeremy nodded.

"Then I'm going over to the guesthouse and on to bed." Paige paused. "Give her my love, will you?"

Jeremy nodded. Paige slipped out the French doors in the family room and walked discreetly around the far side of the swimming pool, toward her temporary residence. Taylor and her parents were so caught up in what they were saying to each other they barely noticed.

Aware there was little he could do except let the private family scene play out, Jeremy waited, pacing the kitchen, until Taylor's parents left. The minute their vehicle drove away, he was out the back door, at her side. Despite the tumultuous events of the evening, she was as lovely as ever. "What did they say?"

Taylor avoided his gaze. "Nothing important."

"They drove several hours out of their way to talk to you," he said carefully, underscoring every word.

Taylor bit into her lower lip. "They're embarrassed about the bad publicity I'm getting."

Jeremy slid his hand beneath her chin and turned her face back to his. "They know it's not true."

A pulse throbbed in Taylor's neck, and she regarded him in silence, clearly wanting to trust him to stand by her in the midst of this growing scandal, but not quite able to. Probably because of the way he had deserted her before…and what her own parents were putting her through now, just showing up like this and lecturing her as if she were an errant child in need of schooling.

Taylor drew a deep breath, oblivious of the way the action raised and lowered the soft swell of her breasts, then released it, just as slowly. "They know I wouldn't sleep with a married man," she revealed cautiously after a moment, doing her best to disguise her hurt.

"Then…?" Jeremy asked gruffly, wishing he could just take her to bed and make love to her until all the sadness and uncertainty in her eyes went away.

Her spine ramrod-straight, Taylor moved away. "They think this scandal is going to hurt you."

Jeremy shifted so she had no choice but to look at him.

"Like hell it will." Assured of her attention, he continued, "This isn't Dallas. The people around here are salt of the earth. They know what's important in life. Made-up Hollywood stories are not even on their radar screen."

"That's what I said!" Taylor sniffed.

"Don't let them upset you."

Taylor brushed one errant strand of hair off her forehead, her emotions a mixture of frustration and despair. "That's easy for you to say." Her customary spunk returned. "Your parents are proud of you." She pointed to his chest. "Hell!" She threw up her hands. "*My* parents are proud of you."

"Your parents are proud of you, too."

"Not the way they would be if I'd become a doctor."

What could he say to that? Sadly, it was as true as it was just plain wrong. The love given to a person should not depend on what she did for a living. Unfortunately, he wasn't sure Taylor's single-minded parents would ever accept that.

He now knew differently. "I'm proud of you," he murmured. And he wasn't just saying that, he meant it from the bottom of his heart.

She tilted her head. "Why?"

He caught her against him once again. "The way you're dealing with all of this, with such grace and dignity. You made a mistake, selling the rights to your book to Zak and Zoe. You won't repeat it. But right now you have to live with it," he told her gently. "I was there today. I know it's not easy…anything but. Yet you're getting through it and you're moving on, and you're going to be an incredibly successful writer despite all this."

Her lips curved into a rueful smile, even as her eyes shone with hope. "From your wish to reality," she whispered.

He pulled her closer still. "Believe in yourself. The way I believe in you." He tunneled his hands in her hair and brought her mouth up to his. She rose on tiptoe, the softness of her body giving new heat and hardness to his. Their tongues twined intimately. Her hands grasped his shoulders, sliding upward to cup his face. He anchored an arm about her waist and shifted her closer still. Feelings poured from his heart, followed swiftly by a need that was soul-deep. No woman had ever touched his heart this way. No woman had ever made him want with such fire and determination. If having her in his arms like this wasn't heaven on earth, he didn't know what was.

She moaned as he shifted a hand beneath her cotton top, gently caressing the skin above her waist. She let out a shuddering sigh. "You're just doing this to make me feel better."

All too willing to let passion lead them where it might, Jeremy concentrated on the delicate shell of her ear, the slope of her neck. "Is it working?" He breathed in the sweetness of her scent.

"Ah…" Smiling, she paused as if she didn't really even have to think about it. "Yes."

He grinned, bending to slip a hand beneath her knees. "Then that's all I need to know." Shifting her up into his arms and against his chest, he carried her into the ranch house, down the hall, to the bedroom where she had been staying. He set her down beside the bed, gathered her close, and began kissing her once again.

Taylor'd thought she could separate love and sex, but as Jeremy continued to kiss and caress her, it all became one and the same. She couldn't make love to him like this, without loving him. She couldn't bare her soul to him, and confide in him, without taking him into her life, into her heart. When they were together like this, all she wanted was to surrender to the possibilities ahead of them. To think about the future—their future—right here in Laramie.

It didn't matter that these hopelessly dependent feelings were quite unlike her, or that she had never behaved so recklessly in her entire life. All she knew for certain was that something fundamental had changed between them, for the better. And that she wanted to be with him, as friends and lovers…as soul mates. And as they moved, naked, to the bed, she was beginning to think that was all Jeremy wanted, too.

The lights were on. His eyes darkened as he took in her soft curves. "Let yourself go," he whispered, stretching out beside her. He stroked the tender insides of her legs, traced the dampness that flowed. His lips ghosted across her ribs, past the flatness of her abdomen. They'd barely started and already she could feel herself sliding inexorably toward the edge. Holding her fast, he brought her even closer. She whispered his name. He murmured hers, all the while touching and exploring, kissing and loving, until they connected with each other irrevocably and the world narrowed to just the two of them.

Aware she wanted so much more than just the feel of his possession, of his hands and lips on her hands and breasts, she shifted, draping herself over him. She wanted to know all of him, wanted to explore, take and give. She wanted to dip her tongue into his navel, show him they didn't need to do anything but feel. Palms sliding over his hips, she lifted him to her, smiling as his body took on an insistent throb all of its own.

She continued to slide over him, acquiescing as he ran his palms across her legs and gently parted her thighs. Their lips fused, as surely as their bodies, and the swiftness of her pinnacle caught them both by surprise. She wanted him. She let him know it. He possessed her slowly, sweetly. Lost in the pleasure, she pressed her breasts against his chest. She gripped his shoulders, hard. He took her to incredible heights. Needing him as she had never needed before, she surrendered her heart, until desire streamed through her like fire, until she felt warm and safe.

The next thing she knew he was shifting, so he was on top

of her. Trembling with a need they no longer wanted to contain, they rocked together toward the outer limits of their control. And then there was no more holding back, no more restraint. They shuddered together in urgent release, connecting in a way they had never known possible.

The aftershocks faded. Jeremy dipped his head and kissed her again. And Taylor knew happiness wasn't just a romantic notion perpetuated in her books. It was real. It was here. It was now. Bliss, for her, was having Jeremy in her life.

For today, tomorrow…and maybe, just maybe—she was beginning to think contentedly—forever.

"GLAD I CAUGHT YOU," Taylor's editor, Geraldine Meyerson, said over the phone Monday morning. "Did you get the *Mr. What If…?* galleys yet?"

"About half an hour ago," Taylor confirmed. "Unfortunately, I have to be at the soundstage today." Otherwise, she'd dive right into them. "They're shooting the beginning and end of the dream sequence on set there. But I'll be able to read the author proofs tomorrow and get back to you with any corrections on Wednesday."

Geraldine paused. "There's been some discussion about what to do with the publication date of your second novel. We're not sure whether to delay it or move it up, given the spate of mostly bad publicity."

Knowing where this line of questioning was going, Taylor said matter-of-factly, "For the record, Geraldine, those stories are not true. I am not having an affair with Zak Townsend."

"What about the cute doctor?"

"He's a friend," she said.

"A rather good friend, I'm guessing, from the photos I've seen of the two of you kissing."

Taylor closed her eyes, wishing for the umpteenth time

that this would all go away. "I don't want to discuss my private life."

"Normally, I wouldn't ask, but Sassy Woman Press needs some forewarning if there is anything else really sensational that's about to be revealed, because that could drastically impact your sales, depending on what the news is."

Taylor appreciated her editor's candor. She spoke frankly, too. "I'm hoping that when the shooting wraps today, Zak and Zoe will return to their recording careers and that will be that until the film comes out."

"The plan was to bring the movie out in the fall but the word in Los Angeles is that the release may be shelved indefinitely, unless the reshooting turns the project around."

Taylor sighed and moved her cell phone to her other ear. "Between you and me, from what I saw yesterday, I wouldn't count on that."

"Our gut instinct is to release both your books ahead of the film. Try to get as much buzz as we can, and let the two works stand on their own, before they are linked with the film. Especially if the movie is a stinker."

And it is, Taylor thought. Restless, she stood and began to pace around. "That sounds good to me."

"But that in turn is dependent upon all this gossip surrounding you and Zak and Zoe Townsend ending, pronto. Can you make that happen?"

Once again, Taylor steeled herself for battle in a publicity war she had never wanted to enter. "I'll do everything in my power to try," she promised.

"ZAK AND ZOE need to see you before you leave," the Townsend publicist told Taylor, at six o'clock that evening. "They're in Zoe's dressing room."

Taylor fervently hoped Zak and Zoe weren't going to make

a demand for more rewrites and/or additional new scenes. She had spent most of the day changing bits of dialogue around—to no real affect, only to change it back again. She was exhausted.

Nevertheless, Taylor picked up her pad and pen, slung her carryall over her shoulder and headed for Zoe's dressing room.

To her dismay, Zak was wearing only the loincloth he'd been garbed in during the beginning of the dreamed love scene—heaven knew what, if anything, he had under it. Meanwhile, Zoe had shed her traditional Indian garb for a fringed buckskin bustier, matching buckskin thong and knee-high moccasins that looked like they had come from a trendy lingerie store that specialized in sexual fantasy.

"We're unhappy with you," Zoe snapped. "We just got a copy of the Laramie newspaper. We saw your interview with the editor. You didn't mention *Sail Away* or how great it was to be working with Zak and me once!"

Zak fumed, "You need to be playing up that angle as much as possible. We're certainly doing our part to drum up interest in the film."

Taylor flashed a brief, officious smile. "I'm sure Brian Hilliard would be glad to interview you for the Laramie newspaper."

"Please!" Zoe paraded back and forth as if she were center stage at one of her pop-rock concerts. "Zak and I don't sit for interviews at newspapers with a circulation of less than half a million!"

"Then I don't see what the problem is," Taylor stated.

"The problem is you should be *grateful* to us for this opportunity we've given you," Zak said. "And we're not feeling it."

That's because such gratitude didn't exist, Taylor thought. Having been reared to be polite and respectful of others no matter what the circumstances, she said, "I apologize for the oversight. I'm sorry if your feelings were hurt. That was not what I intended." What she *had* intended was to do everything she could to save her career—without negatively impacting anyone else's. She hoped she had accomplished that. Or at least made a start of it. No way was she letting these two idiots drag her down into the muck any more than they already had. "So if that's all…?"

"It's not," Zoe said, her gaze shifting to Taylor's midriff. "I want to know if there is any truth to the rumor you're pregnant. And if so, exactly who the father is!"

"THAT WOULD BE ME," Jeremy said from the doorway.

"You'll swear you are the father of Taylor's baby, and no one else!" Zoe regarded him suspiciously.

"Should there be one? Absolutely."

Taylor stared at Jeremy as he strolled into Zoe's dressing room. Was he nuts? Goading Zoe and Zak this way? Especially when he knew the Townsends' lack of common sense was trumped only by their self-absorption?

"We're going to be late if we don't get a move on." Jeremy wrapped a protective arm about Taylor's waist. Taylor leaned into the curve of his body, absorbing his strength.

"Remember what we said about what we expect of you, Taylor," Zoe warned.

Taylor raised her fist in an insincere gesture of solidarity. "Full throttle!"

Jeremy and Taylor walked away. With his arm still around her. "You didn't have to do that," she murmured.

"True." Jeremy adjusted his long strides to her smaller ones. "But consider the alternative."

Taylor cocked her head playfully. "I tell them I'm not pregnant?"

Jeremy chuckled, scrutinizing her flat tummy. "They'll figure that out soon enough. Meanwhile, it gave them something to ponder."

Taylor slipped out from beneath his arm. "Except for one thing, this really isn't your problem."

"The tabloids today say otherwise," he reminded her.

Slowing her pace, Taylor steered clear of a line of thick electrical cables snaking across the cement floor of the soundstage. "*You're* reading them?"

Jeremy stepped past her to open the exit doors. Bright sunlight streamed over them, temporarily making it hard to see. "In self-defense, yeah." He shaded his eyes with his hand. Taylor did the same. As their pupils adjusted, they resumed walking. "I want to know what I've been up to," Jeremy teased. "This seems the only way to find out."

Taylor stuffed her hands in the pockets of her cropped linen pants. "Then you saw the photos of us picking berries?"

"Ticks me off, too. I bought that ranch for privacy."

Taylor drew in a breath, released it slowly. "I keep hoping they'll go away, especially since I hardly ever seem to see the paparazzi taking photos of me."

"All the better to keep us off guard." Jeremy dared another glance at her stomach and cleared his throat. "Speaking of which…"

She held up a hand, well aware of what he was about to say. "If you're referring to Trashtalk.com." She'd seen the embarrassing photos, too. The crew had been looking at them, on the set, whenever Zoe and Zak weren't around.

He shook his head, perplexed, his gaze shifting over her once again. "I don't know how they made your tummy bulge like that."

"Photo retouching? Camera angle?" Taylor guessed miserably.

"Something," he agreed. Then he winked. "Because I can vouch for the fact your abs are as tight as can be."

Her blood heated at the memory of his big square hands moving gently over her body. "You don't have to keep coming to my rescue."

He threaded his way through the vehicles in the studio parking lot. "I know that." His voice was gruff.

Sensing emotion in him, too, she asked, "But…?"

Jeremy stopped where he was, between a car and a pickup truck. He stood, thighs braced apart. His body blocked her path. "If anyone claims to be the father of that baby you're *not* carrying, it's going to be me."

The absurdity of the situation made her laugh. The sheer proximity of him made her catch her breath. "You're taking chivalry to new heights," she teased.

He appreciated her attempt to deflect with humor. His eyes darkened seriously. "I owe you." He framed her face with his hands. "I wasn't gallant when we parted company years ago. I should have been. And while I can't undo that, I can make it up to you now."

Taylor was aware she'd never wanted a *gentleman* more. Suddenly, her heart was racing. "Is that what this is?" she whispered, thrilled by the affectionate look in his eyes.

He nodded, drawing her closer yet. "Among other things."

Taylor let her eyes drift closed. Moments later, she felt his lips on hers again. Contentment sifted through her, followed swiftly by tenderness. Affection. Sensations of lust and love and a connection that went far deeper than any she had ever experienced. He flattened a hand over her spine, bringing her all the closer. She went up on tiptoe, wreathing her arms about his neck. His tongue eased into her mouth, erotically deepening the kiss, bringing them closer yet. Only the knowledge that they were in the parking lot of the studio, in broad daylight, for all to see, kept them from taking it any further.

Reluctantly, they broke it off and breathlessly drew apart. Taylor had only had to look into Jeremy's eyes to know he wanted to make love with her as much as she wanted to make love with him. And yet they'd had no specific plans for this evening, which begged the question... "Why are you here?"

He kept his eyes on hers. "I want to have dinner with you tonight."

Immediately after she accepted his invitation, unease reverberated through her. What if spending the evening together out in public fanned the flames for even more tabloid gossip?

Chapter Ten

Showdown!

The last day of (additional) filming on *Sail Away* was filled with fireworks. Zak and Zoe Townsend battled back, amidst mounting rumors of infidelity, betrayal and pregnancy. The tension culminated in a dressing-room contretemps between Zoe, Zak, and Zak's purported mistress, scribe Taylor O'Quinn. Ms. O'Quinn refused to take responsibility for the failures on the troubled set, while her lover-in-the-wings, Dr. Jeremy Carrigan, arrived just in time to claim paternity of Ms. O'Quinn's baby.

Movie Talk Magazine
June 10

"If you look over your shoulder one more time," Jeremy drawled from the other side of the booth in Sonny's Barbecue restaurant, "I think you're going to have to throw some salt. Either that or get diagnosed with self-con-scious-itis."

Taylor grinned at the fictional malady and ran her hand contemplatively across the burgundy oilcloth table covering. "What's the cure for that?"

Jeremy mopped up the last bit of sauce with a thick slice of Texas toast. He waggled his brows at her. "Come back to the ranch with me and I'll show you."

Taylor chuckled despite herself. "Which ranch?"

He shrugged his broad shoulders affably. "Whichever one you please."

Taylor considered her options. "Then it'll be the Chamberlain ranch, cause I'd really like to soak in the pool for a bit before I get started on those galleys."

He signaled for the waitress and ordered pie for them both. Pecan a la mode for her, sweet potato with whipped cream for him. "Sounds good to me," he said after the waitress had replenished their iced teas and walked away. "I have to tell Paige I'm moving out by the end of the week, in any case."

Taylor paused, her fork hovering just above her plate. "Not before then?"

"I admit I'm procrastinating again."

"Because?" Taylor asked.

"I like living with you and don't want that to end."

There was a cure for that. But Taylor knew it was too soon for them to be talking about moving in together. She had done that before, with Bart because she wanted—needed—to feel safe. And because it was convenient. She knew on the surface it probably looked like she was doing exactly the same thing with Jeremy. For a whole lot of reasons he still knew nothing about, that wasn't the case.

"What are you thinking?" he prodded in a gruffly tender voice that said she could tell him anything and he would understand.

But Taylor didn't know how to broach the truth. Didn't know how he would feel if he ever discovered that he had been unwittingly immortalized. "That I'm going to have to swim about one hundred laps if I want to work off all the calories

I consumed at dinner this evening," she fibbed. Everything from the coleslaw, to the potato salad, to the brisket and barbecued ribs, had been delicious.

"I know what you mean." Jeremy patted his full stomach. "The food in Texas is amazing." He turned his head as Krista Sue Wright walked up to their table.

"Hey, doc. Taylor," she said with a smile.

"Krista Sue," Jeremy replied.

"What's up?" Taylor asked. It was clear from the expression on her face that Krista Sue wanted to talk to them about something.

Jeremy rose halfway out of his seat, already making room. "Do you want to join us?" he asked, as gentlemanly as ever.

"No." Krista Sue gestured for them both to stay seated. "Brian will be in shortly. He's parking the car. I just thought I'd come over and say hi and tell you I didn't take the job with Jenna after all. It was just too much of a risk. And it was silly, really," Krista Sue rushed on, shaking her head, "when you consider how long I've dreamed of being in a classroom. As Brian pointed out, I just spent four years and thousands of dollars in college tuition learning how to be a teacher. I really should use that skill now and get some experience before deciding I don't want to do it after all. And sewing will always be a hobby for me."

Brian walked up to join her. Oblivious to the subject of the conversation, he looked as content as his fiancée was conflicted. "I'm glad we ran into you-all," Brian addressed Taylor and Jeremy. "I just had a phone call from a friend in Dallas."

"WHAT DO YOU THINK IT MEANS?" Jeremy asked Taylor, when they left the barbecue restaurant and headed out to their vehicles in the parking lot. He repeated the news Brian Hilliard had conveyed, via his friend at the Dallas newspaper. "Zoe and Zak are shopping a story about their current travails?"

"I imagine it's an extension of their current drive for publicity for *Sail Away*." Taylor lounged next to the driver door of her Jeep. "They're trumping me by going to a bigger newspaper. I predict that in retribution, they'll talk about the process of turning a sow's ear into a silk purse."

He folded his arms over the hard muscles of his chest. "Meaning, in their view, your book sucked and they've been working overtime to fix it."

"Right. Hence covering themselves should it flop as badly as everyone thinks it will."

"That makes sense." Jeremy ran a hand beneath his jaw, caressing the evening beard that made him look even more ruggedly handsome than ever.

"In their view, I'm expendable. And the worse things get…"

Jeremy took her hand in his. "The more they are liable to do everything they can to put your head on the chopping block, instead of theirs," he guessed.

"Exactly." Taylor savored the warmth of Jeremy's touch. "Unfortunately, there's nothing I can do about it now."

His fingers tightened around hers. "You could go public with your own story."

Taylor withdrew her hand and stepped back with a frown. "First of all, I haven't been paid the rest of my advance money for the film rights and screenplay. Second, if I were to say one word against them they'd use every ounce of influence they have in the business to ruin me. And I can't afford the legal fees."

She hadn't told Paige or Jeremy, but she was down to her last couple hundred dollars in her checking account. She hated being dependent on the kindness of friends. She could go to her family for money and lodging, but she really didn't want her parents—who already doubted her—to find out how dire her straits were. They'd probably just raise the issue of her attending medical school again…and that was the *last* thing she needed.

"No." Taylor lifted a staying hand and paced back and forth beside her SUV. "What I need to do is keep my head down and my flak jacket on and wait this out."

Jeremy nodded, outwardly accepting her decision. And yet the look in his eyes…

"You think I should fight them on this, don't you?"

He shrugged. "Walking away from a bully—and Zoe and Zak are two of the worst bullies I've ever seen—never works. At best, you get a temporary reprieve, but they keep coming back again…until you stand up to them."

Taylor knew Jeremy was right, in certain respects. On others… She swallowed hard and briefly avoided his probing gaze. "The one thing I have going for me is their short attention span. Both are set to start working on new music videos to coincide with the release of their new CDs by the end of the week, so hopefully their attention will be directed back to the music business by then."

Jeremy smiled. "I hope for your sake it is. In the meantime, do you still plan to start reading your galleys this evening?"

"Yes. I want to do as much as I can tonight." She knew it would help get her mind off the mess her life had become. "I promised my editor I'd get the corrections back to her as soon as possible." And work always cheered her up. "Are you headed back to the Chamberlain ranch now, too?"

He shook his head. "I think since you're going to be working I'll spend the night at my ranch. That way I won't be tempted to distract you. And it'll give me a chance to get more work done there."

She thought about what kind of change this signified. "Seriously?"

Jeremy clasped her shoulders with one arm, drawing her

close. He brushed a light kiss across her temple. "It's time I made Lago Vista Ranch a home."

"How ARE THE GALLEYS GOING?" Jeremy asked Taylor late the following afternoon.

"I finished about half an hour ago and mailed the corrections in to my editor." Which meant she was completely free for the evening.

"Want to have dinner with me again tonight?" he asked.

She had been hoping Jeremy would ask. "Love to. Just tell me when and where."

"Lago Vista Ranch. Seven o'clock."

Figuring she would surprise Jeremy with homemade biscuits and some of the blackberry jam she had made that afternoon, Taylor went into the kitchen and whipped up some dough. Figuring they could bake the buttermilk biscuits in his toaster oven, she put the flour-dusted rounds into a plastic container for transport and went to get ready for their date. That all took a little longer than anticipated. Hence, she did not arrive at Lago Vista Ranch until almost seven fifteen. His pickup truck was not there and he didn't answer the doorbell.

Which was strange. It was as unlike him to be late as it was her. Worried they might have gotten their signals crossed, she tried him on his cell. He wasn't answering. She walked around the outside of the ranch house, appreciating the improvements that had been made, including some plantation-style shutters in the wing that housed the master bedroom.

Without warning, Taylor felt the back of her neck prickle. She had the acute sensation of being watched. Yet when she turned around and surveyed the landscape, she saw nothing but freshly mown grass, and trees.

She shook the uneasiness off. This tabloid coverage was making her paranoid, that's all. Fortunately, mere seconds later, the sound of a motor vehicle could be heard, making its way up the gravel driveway. Taylor watched as Jeremy's truck came into view. He parked next to her SUV and climbed out.

"Sorry I'm late," he stated cheerfully. He circled around the back and lifted out a cardboard box containing a simple charcoal grill, another containing a starter chimney, and a bag of charcoal. "I had to make a house call on the way here."

"Can I help?"

Looking as thrilled about the evening ahead of them as she was, he handed her two sacks of groceries. "You can carry this."

Together, they started toward the ranch house. "Did you see anyone when you drove up?" Taylor asked.

"No." He gave her a sidelong look and she knew they were both thinking the same thing. "Why?"

She struggled to remain serene. "I had the feeling I was being watched."

He exhaled slowly. "Not surprising, given what we've been through the last ten days or so, but no, I didn't see any cars." He scanned the landscape again just to be sure, as did Taylor. Again, she saw nothing.

"I'm sure I'm just imagining things." With effort, Taylor shook off her distress. She waited while he set down the box and unlocked the front door. "I gather we're grilling out tonight?"

He held the door for her and picked up the box again. "If I can get this thing put together. Otherwise, it's going to be scrambled eggs on the hot plate." He glanced at the picnic hamper she had looped over one arm. "What's in there?"

She sent him a flirtatious glance from beneath her lashes. "Jam—from the blackberries we picked the other day—and homemade biscuits ready to be put in the toaster oven."

He gave her a salacious wink. "If you're thinking the way to my heart is through my stomach…you're right."

He followed her into the ranch house. The work-in-progress was blessedly cool, thanks to the newly installed central air-conditioning.

The cell phone attached to Jeremy's belt began to ring. He looked at the screen, dutiful physician once again. "Sorry. I have to get this." He put the phone to his ear. "Hi, Brian. What's up? Does Krista Sue have her migraine medicine with her? When did she take it? It'll be at least another twenty or thirty minutes before it really takes effect. If she's not better in half an hour, call me back, but if she thinks this is just a run of the mill migraine, my guess is that's all it is. No problem. Take care." Jeremy hung up the phone, looking frustrated.

Taylor couldn't blame him.

Jeremy picked up the box and carted it all the way into the "family room" before setting it down. "Krista Sue was over at the middle school, at a teacher meeting, when a rather severe migraine struck. Fortunately, she was able to take her medicine and keep it down, so my sense is another thirty minutes lying down on a cot in the nurse's office at the school and she'll be fine again." Jeremy ripped open the box containing the grill. "Or at least as fine as she'll be operating under such an enormous stress load. I just don't understand why she didn't take that job with my aunt Jenna."

"You heard what she said last night, when we ran into her. Brian is pressuring her to keep the teaching position." Taylor stowed the groceries in the fridge and returned to help Jeremy extricate the grill pieces from bubble wrap and plastic sheeting.

Jeremy walked over to the toolbox in the corner, to retrieve a flathead screwdriver and a pair of pliers. "Which doesn't make sense. Everyone can see how much Brian loves Krista Sue. Why wouldn't he want what's best for her?"

"Maybe she hasn't told him how much she wants a career as a seamstress."

Jeremy unfolded the instructions for the grill. "Why

wouldn't Krista Sue be honest and open with Brian—if she loves him enough to marry him?"

Taylor sat back on her haunches. "Krista Sue needs Brian to respect her. Obviously, she feels that a career as a seamstress—even for a highly sought after designer like Jenna Lockhart—is somehow inferior to the one she could have as a schoolteacher. Krista Sue may even fear Brian would end their engagement if she chooses one over the other."

Jeremy carried the finished grill through the sliding glass doors, out onto the adjacent stone patio. "That's ridiculous."

"Is it?" Taylor followed with the bag of charcoal.

Silence fell between them. "We're not talking about Brian and Krista Sue anymore, are we?" Jeremy asked, studying her.

"All I'm saying is that I understand how hard it is for Krista Sue to follow a dream not everyone thinks is laudable."

Jeremy lit a match, tossed it onto the coals and stepped back. "Because you did that when you were her age."

Taylor turned and walked toward the door. "I was rejected by nearly all my family and friends. Only Paige seemed to understand what I was going through, and that was probably as much due to the fact that her parents were in the entertainment industry as it was to her innate sensitivity to my desire to be a writer."

Jeremy went straight to the sink to wash his hands. "I'm sorry I didn't support you."

Taylor lounged next to him, her arms folded in front of her. "I am, too. I could have used your friendship during the five lean years I was trying to get published."

Finished, he dried his hands and took her into his arms. "But the disapproval worked in my favor, too. It made me even more determined to succeed. And if there's one thing a writer needs in spades, it's steely resolve."

"I'm proud of the success you've achieved. And I'm

ashamed of the way I let things end between us back then."
He looked into her eyes. "The fact I wasn't there for you the
way I should have been."

She went up on tiptoe. "You're here for me now." That was
all that counted. "The past is over, Jeremy. We have to let it
go. Concentrate on right now."

"And the future." He gathered her closer still, bent his head
and indulged in a tender caress. She knew it was just a kiss,
albeit a very slow, sensual thorough one, but he might as well
have already been making love to her. A torrent of need
whipped through her, sending all her senses into an uproar.

The mood was abruptly broken when Jeremy lifted his
head, looked in the direction of the windows and swore.

JEREMY LET HER GO and stepped back. "We're not alone."

She caught his glance and deliberately did not look away.
"Papparazzi?"

He cupped her shoulders, the warmth of his palms trans-
mitting through the cap sleeves of her sheer white blouse to
her skin. "The same lady that's been following us. What do
you say we put on a show that will keep her here, clandes-
tinely snapping away, while we wait for the sheriff's department to arrive?"

Determined to get the snooping photographer out of their
lives, whatever it took, Taylor drew a bolstering breath. "I'm
game if you are," she whispered, brushing her fingertips
across his chest.

Jeremy caught her hand and brought it to his lips for a brief,
smoldering kiss. He ran his other hand lightly down her spine,
to the small of her back. His grip tightened possessively. "First
things first. We have to act like I didn't spot her and kiss again."

A wave of desire coursed through Taylor. "Like this?" She
wrapped her arms about his neck.

He buried his face in the fragrant softness of her just-washed hair. "Very nice," he murmured seductively, kindling her senses all the more.

Loving how intimate and cozy it felt to be here like this, even if they did have an unwanted audience, she cuddled closer. "Now what?" she teased.

"We turn our heads at the same time, as if the phone is ringing. On three." Jeremy counted soft and low. They broke apart abruptly, and he plucked his cell phone off the kitchen counter. Mischief dancing in his eyes, he commanded, "Toss your head and look ticked off. Like you can't believe I'd allow an interruption at such a tender moment."

"No problem." Purposefully keeping her back toward the windows, to visually compromise any photo being taken, Taylor adopted a highly indignant posture.

Pretending to ignore Taylor, Jeremy picked up the phone, punched a number and put it toward his ear. "I'd like to report a trespasser. Lago Vista Ranch. Thanks." He cut the connection, swung back around, his eyes reassuring, his mouth grim. "They said they've already got a patrol car in the area. Deputies Kevin McCabe and Rio Vasquez should be here in about fifteen minutes."

"So now what?" Taylor murmured.

"First, you resist me," Jeremy schooled, taking her in his arms once again. Taylor splayed her hands across his chest and turned her head sharply to one side. He lowered his lips to the delicate shell of her ear. "And we pretend to make out while I try to get a look out the windows."

She shivered in reaction to the thrill of his lips kissing a path from ear to throat. Beneath her tank top, her nipples tightened. "See anything?" she gasped as he kissed the hollow of her throat, before making his way to her other ear.

"She's still there, hiding behind the trees, appears to have a camera with a telephoto lens." Jeremy swore again as he reported with a mixture of surprise and frustration, "She appears to be removing said lens and packing up to leave."

"Then we'll have to give her incentive to stay," Taylor vowed, pretending to smack him across the face.

"Ow!" Jeremy dramatically rubbed the jaw her hand had barely grazed. He stepped back, knowing it was his turn to appear indignant. "What was that for?" he demanded, acting peeved.

Taylor struggled not to smile at the twinkle in his eyes. "I don't know," she told him, determined to keep the prying photographer there long enough for the police to catch her in the act. "I'm making it up as I go."

Jeremy swiftly caught Taylor's wrist and held it aloft—as if to prevent her from slapping him again. "And it's working, because that telephoto lens just got put right back on," he reported. "How about throwing something at my head?"

"How's this?" She picked up a stack of medical journals.

He ducked, but not before one hit him in the shoulder. "Nice." He held his hands aloft, ready, should she hurl another. "Try it again."

Taylor gave another a Frisbee-style whirl. "These photos could end up in the tabloid, you know." She ducked as he tossed one back at her.

He mugged in frustration at the missed shot. "Not if the sheriff's department gets ahold of her camera and it becomes evidence in an ongoing criminal investigation, they won't."

Taylor turned her back to the windows once again. "Ah. Good point."

Jeremy aimed a thumb at his chest. "But first, I want to know why that woman keeps dogging you and me! Certainly there are more glamorous celebrities she could trail." In full command of the situation, Jeremy took Taylor in his arms again and looked down at her. "Probably," he continued, tenderly smoothing the hair from her face and tucking it behind her ear, "for a lot more money."

Basking in the gentleness of his touch, Taylor could almost…believe a miracle had happened…that he was falling in love with her as much as she was falling in love with him.

"I've been wondering why that woman is so fixated on us myself," Taylor whispered, fully acknowledging that she had never desired anyone more. And then Jeremy's head was lowering and their lips met in a searing kiss that banished all rational thoughts from her mind.

As the heated kiss lingered on, Taylor wrapped her hands around Jeremy's neck, pressed her body close to his and kissed him back with everything she had. The two of them could have stayed that way forever, probably would have, had it not been for the sudden, sharp rapping on the window.

Brought swiftly back to reality, she and Jeremy broke apart and looked over into the grinning face of Deputy Rio Vasquez. Out behind the trees, Kevin McCabe was busying cuffing the fifty-something paparazzo and reciting her Miranda rights.

"SHE'S GIVING US A STORY," Deputy Rio Vasquez reported minutes later, after conferring once again with his partner. "Her ID says her name is Ilene Wells, but the driver's license isn't coming up on our system as valid, so we're taking her in."

"What has she told you?" Taylor asked curiously, watching as Kevin McCabe escorted her over to the back of the squad car and waited for her to get settled in the rear seat behind the barricade, before speaking into his radio once again.

Kevin shut the rear car door, while Rio continued the update. "She says she wandered onto Lago Vista Ranch by mistake and thought the ranch house so unusual she decided to take a few photos of it. She *claims* she had no idea anyone would actually want to live in such a weird-looking place."

"Gotta agree with her there," Jeremy admitted reluctantly, running a hand through his hair. "If I hadn't wanted to have my own ranch—and liked the lake view so much—there's no way I would have selected this house, either."

Rio shrugged. "It's a diamond in the rough," he offered with a wink. "Like a lot of us."

"Did she explain why she was also on Beau Chamberlain's ranch, snapping photos of us?"

"She says she's a fan of his and hoped to meet him. She also admitted she's been roaming the area, camera in hand, trying to locate other celebrities who happen to be around."

"Like Zak and Zoe Townsend," Taylor enthused, not buying the coincidental excuse for an instant.

Rio nodded. "In any case, the sheriff's department can hold Ms. Whatever-Her-Real-Name-Is up to seventy-two hours while we check out her story, see if there are any outstanding warrants out on her. My feeling—from talking to her—is that she's no amateur. She doesn't seem all that worried about getting caught out here. In fact, she seems confident she'll get out of this jam, as well as any charges that she has been stalking you."

Which meant what? Taylor wondered. That someone was out to get her? Or out to get Zak and Zoe and she—and now Jeremy—had just happened to get drawn into the ugly mess because of proximity to the pop-rockers?

"You'll keep us posted?" Jeremy said, his expression thoughtful, too. "Let us know what turns up?"

Rio nodded.

At the squad car, Deputy Kevin McCabe waved, signaling he was ready to take their suspect back to the sheriff's station.

"Meanwhile," Rio advised devilishly, "you two go back to what you were doing." He was still chuckling as he strode off.

Jeremy turned to Taylor, gauging her reaction.

"You know," she said dryly. "I'd never been a woman with a 'reputation' until I met you."

Jeremy did not look the least bit sorry he had kissed her the way he had earlier. Nor could she say she was either. "I never had a rep, either," he confessed, wrapping his arm about her shoulders and looking like he wanted to kiss her again. "And now I've got one, too."

Chapter Eleven

Zak and Zoe Defy Attempt To Split Them Up!

"I don't blame Taylor O'Quinn for being attracted to my husband," Zoe Townsend admitted, as she sat down for an interview in the penthouse suite of the Dallas hotel. "Tons of women are, and why not, he's gorgeous and sexy and talented!" Zoe reached over and lovingly squeezed Zak's hand. "But Ms. O'Quinn needs to understand that her attempts to break us up and steal Zak away from me were never going to work."

"My heart belongs to Zoe," Zak said, looking deep into his beloved's eyes. "It always has, it always will…"

In Tune magazine
June 11

"Hard to believe I owned this property for two years before sitting here like this," Jeremy said several hours later, taking her hand in his.

The remains of their dinner and the bottle of wine they had shared had been packed away. Their stomachs were full, and it would be dark in another half an hour or so. Yet they were reluctant to leave the blanket they had spread out on the ridge, overlooking Lake Laramie. She looked at him curiously. "You've never brought anyone here for dinner? Or never sat here enjoying the view of the setting sun over the lake?"

He lifted her hand and kissed the inside of her wrist. "I haven't done either."

Skin tingling warmly at the brief but tender caress, Taylor studied him. He looked so handsome in the tropical print shirt, and loose slacks. Like a sophisticate on a Hawaiian vacation rather than a gentleman rancher. "Why not?" She kissed the inside of his wrist, too.

"A lot of reasons." He drew her back on the blanket, and lay down beside her. He rolled onto his side and propped his head on his upraised hand. His dark brown eyes took on an intimate sheen. "I never found anyone who could see the raw beauty of Lago Vista or share my vision of what this ranch could be one day."

Taylor tried not to think how much she wanted him…how much she wanted to stay here forever, just like this. She was really getting ahead of herself here. "You probably just didn't try hard enough," she teased.

All the humor left his face. "I was the laughingstock of all of Laramie County. It would have been one thing, had I planned to raise livestock, grow landscape plants here or let 'em prospect for oil."

"But you didn't do any of those things." Taylor reflected out loud.

He shook his head. "I think, in retrospect, I was waiting for you to come along."

She caught her breath and sat up. "Don't say things like that."

He stayed where he was. "Why not?"

Taylor looked over her shoulder at him. "Because we both know it isn't true." She'd fooled herself once, where he was concerned, wishing for more than was actually possible from him. She did not want to do it again. "You didn't have any idea I'd be back when you bought this property. I didn't have the slightest suspicion I'd return." And she'd certainly had no clue when she did she would fall headlong into his arms and discover the kind of passion that had once only been a wistful fantasy…

He sat up slowly, too. Thoughtfully, he traced the crinkled cotton of the skirt draping her calves. "Or in other words, the only reason you're even in Laramie…is because Paige is living here again."

Emotion clogging her throat, Taylor nodded. It didn't mean she hadn't thought of Jeremy in the intervening years. She had, more than he knew. "Right." Fearful she was about to reveal too much, she turned her gaze back to the sun setting slowly over the lake, in a pink and red-streaked summer sky.

"That guy—the rebound person you wrote about in your first novel—he really broke your heart, didn't he?"

Taylor shrugged, not sure she should get into this in detail with him, for fear of what she would inadvertently give away. As the tension-filled silence between them drew out, Jeremy looked so ticked off at this nameless someone she found herself saying, "It wasn't his fault."

Jeremy swore, disagreeing. "That rebound guy sent you into the arms of Baywatch Bart!"

"Bart was very good to me. He just didn't love me the way I needed to be loved, and to be fair, I didn't love him enough, either." Their relationship had been a necessary rite of passage, for both of them. "Bart and I are better for having known each other. And we're happier apart. End of story."

Jeremy appeared to consider that. "And yet," he noted eventually, tracing a path from her calf to her knee, "you're still extremely skittish when it comes to you and me."

She was skittish, Taylor acknowledged, because Jeremy

meant too much to her, because he had the capacity to hurt her like no one else ever had. And she didn't want to have her heart crushed to pieces yet again. "I admit, sometimes what we've found the last couple of weeks seems almost too good to be true." Like something she dreamed up and wrote about. Not something that actually happened.

"But it isn't." His hand edged higher still, stalling out at midthigh.

She swallowed. "It's early in the relationship." Right now she was still a success. She hadn't disappointed him. What would happen if her publisher decided not to publish her second book at all and/or reissue her first, because of all the bad publicity? What if all she had was a column in the *Laramie Press?* Or worst case scenario, what if Brian Hilliard decided she was too controversial a figure to employ and she was completely unemployed? Would Jeremy still want her in his life then? A lot of people wanted a successful person around. Few people embraced the person who was perceived a failure.

Pushing away the fear of the unknown, she forced herself to continue. "A lot can happen."

"You're right about that." He studied her briefly. "You could move in with me. Have an entire wing to yourself. I admit," he held up a hand before she could catch her breath and interrupt, "it's not fixed up now, but it will be, probably by the end of the summer. In the meantime, you'd have a quiet place to work on your next book, or your newspaper column, or whatever."

Taylor looked at him in shock. "Are you asking me to be your roommate…or your lover?" she asked finally.

His smile widened. "Both."

JEREMY KNEW, even before he had finished making the proposition, that it had been the wrong thing to say. He had brought

Taylor out here, to have dinner on the ridge overlooking the lake, because it was the most romantic spot on the entire ranch.

He had intended to tell her he was in love with her. Crazy, wildly, passionately in love.

He wanted to know if she felt the same.

Her skittish attitude toward their relationship had him backing off.

His need to have her in his life in a lasting, meaningful way had him throwing out the idea of moving in together. Sharing space. It was the best way, the fastest way he knew to get as close to Taylor as he wanted to be.

Yet he knew from the quiet look of disappointment on her face that asking her this had been a mistake.

Now that the words were out there, he couldn't act as if he hadn't meant them. He had.

"I want to be with you," he told her softly, wrapping his arms around her. "I've waited too long, been apart from you too long, to let you walk away." He swallowed around the thickening in his throat. "At least promise you'll think about it," he said quietly.

Distress mingled with the desire in her blue eyes. "Jeremy—"

Wanting, needing, to show her how right they could be together, Jeremy bent his head and captured her lips with his. "I can't imagine my life without you, Taylor," he whispered, feeling her surrender against him.

Keeping her wrapped in the cradle of his arms, their lips still fused together, he lowered her gently to the blanket once again. They stretched out on their sides. She arced against him, their mouths hungry, her breasts pressed against the hardness of his chest. The sweet, indulgent kiss went on and on until she offered herself to him completely, giving him the kind of access to her heart and soul he'd longed to have. He kissed her again, delving into her mouth with his tongue, in a rhythm of penetration and retreat, until there was no doubt for either of them about what he wanted, or what was coming next.

She trembled as he opened the buttons of her sheer white blouse and eased it off. He pushed her tank top up, revealing the flushed curves of her breasts and taut rosy nipples. The intoxicating scent of her filling his senses, he lowered his head and captured the softness of her skin with his lips. She moaned and caught his head in her hands as he suckled gently, then moved lower still. Easing a hand beneath the flowing fabric of her skirt, he removed the thong and caressed the silky-soft insides of her thighs. His own body throbbing, the darkness of night descending on them, he loved her slowly, thoroughly, until she was quivering from head to toe, arching her back, and moaning soft and low in her throat. Unable to get enough of her, he moved upward, kissing his way back to her lips, then plunged his tongue inside her mouth. The searing kiss was enough to send her over the edge, and she strained against him, shuddering. "My turn," she whispered, shuddering again.

And then she was sliding over him, unbuttoning his shirt, spreading the fabric wide, using the palms of her hands to generate scorching heat that started at his pecs and slid across his abdomen. Lower still, she found his fly and eased that open, too. The softness of her hands combined with the skill of her fingers to create a firestorm of heat. Wanting her— now—he reached for her. She swept his hands away and focused on her goal, the softness of her mouth creating pleasure that was stunning and all-encompassing.

He caught her to him, shifting her onto her back, and raining kisses down her neck, throat, breasts. Then he lifted her against him and surged inside.

Taylor had wanted to be in complete command of their lovemaking this evening. A futile ambition, as it turned out, for neither of them was in charge of the feelings that spiraled swiftly out of control every time they were together like this. She felt the strength of their passion as she opened herself up to his possession and closed around the hot, hard length of him. She felt it in his gentle kiss and tender caresses, in the exquisite need that drove them both. She might not know what the future held, but she knew what this—what Jeremy—meant to her, and that was everything.

Their hearts thundered in unison as she urged him to go deeper, harder still. And then all doubt faded. They soared ever higher, vaulting into an explosive pleasure unlike anything they had ever known. And as they clung together, gasping, Taylor knew at long last that she was right where she wanted to be, for now...and forever. All they had to do to be happy was make sure that nothing about their relationship or expectations of each other changed.

And that meant no rushing toward a commitment neither of them was ready for, she schooled herself firmly, no premature declarations of love, and especially no moving in together.

All that would come, she was certain of it, as long as they remained patient and took it one slow but careful step at a time.

"MOVING OUT FOR GOOD, hmm?" Paige said the following evening.

Jeremy layered work clothes on hangers across the back of the rear seat in his extended cab pickup truck. Maybe it was part of being one of four kids, but he had never had a problem waiting for what he wanted, especially in situations when biding his time had resulted in him getting exactly what he wanted in the end.

He no longer felt that way.

Having Taylor back in his life had made him realize how much he had been missing, all these years they had been apart. It made him want to make up for lost time—be together as much as possible. Now. Without delay. Because his feelings were not going to change.

That said, he knew it was too soon to be talking marriage. Taylor clearly wasn't ready for that big a step. He honored that. Which was why he had asked her to move in. He'd thought— hoped—that would be a halfway measure that would please them both.

Unfortunately, it'd had the opposite effect on Taylor.

She seemed as drawn to him as ever, yet more cautious about the future.

Nevertheless, there were things he had to do. Like stop living in limbo. Take full possession of the property he had purchased. And make it into a dream home worthy of a woman like Taylor.

Aware Paige was still waiting for his answer, Jeremy shot her an offhand look. "It had to happen sometime. When is your house going to be ready to move into?"

"Another week or two, depending on the installation of the major appliances." Paige turned to Taylor, who stood, waiting to hand over another twelve shirts on hangers. "What about you? Have you decided where you're going to settle next?"

"I've been trying to get her to move in with me," Jeremy said nonchalantly. "Although so far she hasn't given me an answer."

Paige turned to Taylor, brow lifted, and waited for her reaction.

To Jeremy's frustration, Taylor made no effort to further clarify her position. "As much as I appreciated the invitation," she said politely, "I'm not sure I'm ready to live with anyone again just yet."

Not sure how something so simple had gotten so complicated, Jeremy reached for another load and packed it in his truck. "You've been living with both Paige and me for the last two weeks, and it's been fine." *More than fine.*

Both women stiffened. Paige and Taylor exchanged the kind of woman-to-woman glance that always left Jeremy feeling excluded. "This is a little different and you know it," Paige stated finally.

Taylor nodded. "It's kind of like being at Club Chamberlain. Speaking of which," she handed Jeremy another bunch of clothes on hangers before turning back to Paige, "when are your parents getting back from Montana?"

"Another week." Paige paused, getting the reason for Taylor's concern. "You know, I've got a guest room, too," Paige offered, "so if you want to bunk with me at my house when I move back in, Taylor, you're more than welcome to do that, too."

"Hey. Stop giving her other options," Jeremy teased, only half kidding. "I asked first."

Again, the two women exchanged a look. Jeremy had the feeling that Taylor was drifting further away from him than ever.

"Speaking of asking for something," Paige looked at Taylor, "are you going to lend me the galleys of your new book as promised?"

"I'll get it for you." Taylor disappeared into the ranch house.

Jeremy turned to Paige. "Seriously. I could do without the competition. I'm trying to convince her I'm in this for the long haul."

Paige rolled her eyes. "I can see that. I think you're going about it in the entirely wrong way."

"Taylor has lived with a guy before," he pointed out grumpily.

"Exactly." Paige looked at him like he was beyond dumb. "And if you've read her first novel in its entirety, you know why she'll never do it again."

That was the problem, Jeremy reflected. He had stopped reading the novel after a couple of chapters because he hadn't liked thinking about her with another guy, and the hero in the book bore a striking physical resemblance to Baywatch Bart.

Jeremy was sophisticated and physically fit, but he hadn't grown up summering along the Atlantic seaboard, sunning himself on a yacht.

He didn't know how to compete with guys like that. Nor had he ever had the slightest desire to do so. Until now. The thought that Taylor might still be carrying a torch for the guy, or someone just like Bart, rankled—almost as much as her refusal to tell him the real life identity of the Rebound Guy who had inspired her first novel. Especially when his every instinct told him that the guy who had broken Taylor's heart was somehow still standing in the way of his own relationship with her.

"Want to go out to my ranch?" he asked Taylor, when she had joined them again. "We could have dinner by the lake again." Out of politeness, Jeremy looked at Paige. "You can come, too."

Clearly realizing that three would be a crowd, Paige held up the galleys of Taylor's new novel. "Thanks, but I've got a hot date with a very good book." Paige took off for a chaise by the pool, eyes already on the first page.

Watching her go, Taylor blushed with what seemed to be a mixture of embarrassment and pleasure.

"About this evening…?" Jeremy prodded, not about to give up.

To his disappointment, Taylor shook her head. "I've got to work on my first column for the *Laramie Press*. I told Brian Hilliard I'd have it to him by tomorrow morning." She paused. "Maybe tomorrow night instead."

As disappointed as he was, Jeremy knew her request was not unreasonable. "Seven o'clock?"

Taylor gave him a brief kiss on the lips. "It's a date."

JEREMY HUNG UP HIS CLOTHES in the closet, ate the sandwich and slaw he'd brought back with him and then took what was left of his cold beer outside.

   Aware how lonely it was out there without Taylor, he surveyed the property then went back inside. He'd brought the copy of Taylor's first novel with him. Figuring it might give him some clues as to what was going on with her now, he sat down, opened it up to where he'd left off and began to read.

   The further he went in the book, the more his interest grew.

   At the beginning of the story, the heroine was afraid to go after a career as a restaurateur and instead stayed with a retail sales job. The heroine's relationship with Baywatch Bart was filled with hot sex, friendship…and little else. And though ultimately it gave her the platform from which to pursue her dreams, it also created a well of loneliness and disillusionment inside her.

   By the end of the story, when the heroine broke up with Baywatch Bart, it seemed like the right move for both of them. The two remained friends, probably because in the book—as in Taylor's real life—the hero had been using the heroine as a security blanket, too. The heroine had no longer been afraid to go after what she really wanted, to take risks. Jeremy saw that was what Taylor was doing now. She was not going to settle for "almost right" if she could have it all. This time, like her heroine, she was looking for love, commitment, passion—and acceptance.

   Maybe even marriage.

   And all he had offered Taylor was a room in a ranch house that was still one heck of a work-in-progress.

Chapter Twelve

Lose The Wedding Ring…Choose Me!

Friends who were hoping Taylor O'Quinn's crush on pop-rocker Zak Townsend is a thing of the past, have new reason to worry. Seems the hero of Ms. O'Quinn's second chick-lit novel—a story about a woman who refuses to give up on the man she is obsessing over until she lands him for herself—is based on Zak. When asked to comment, Zak and Zoe Townsend said, "We can only *hope* this is not the case…"

CelebrityDreamDates.com
June 12

Taylor was seated in the Chamberlain ranch house kitchen early the next morning, putting the final touches on her column for the Laramie newspaper, when her cell phone rang.

"We've got a problem," Geraldine Meyerson told Taylor, cutting straight to the chase. "Is your computer on?"

"Yes." Apprehension over what she might find stiffened Taylor's shoulders.

"Check your e-mail." Taylor's editor waited while Taylor

hit the speaker button on her phone to free up her hands and accessed her message in-box.

"See the link I sent you?" Geraldine continued, as the back door opened and Jeremy strode in. Although he looked freshly shaved and showered, he was dressed in running shorts and a T-shirt. He carried a clean rumpled dress shirt, slacks and tie, on a hanger.

"Click on it," Geraldine continued, oblivious to the fact there were now three people in on this conversation. "It'll take you to CelebrityDreamDates.com."

Figuring sooner or later Jeremy would hear about whatever this was, Taylor did as instructed and read the latest gossip being reported.

"You know that's not true!" she said, upset about what was being claimed.

Jeremy came around to look over her shoulder. He frowned as he studied what was on the screen.

"I did not model my novel's hero on Zak Townsend!" Taylor said, blushing fiercely, and wishing she'd had the foresight not to turn on the speaker after all.

Geraldine pressed, "But it was a real person, wasn't it?"

On that, Taylor was taking the Fifth. She had a right not to incriminate herself. Or embarrass anyone else, either.

"Because I explicitly remember," Geraldine continued, "when we were talking about the book's theme of unrequited love that you said—"

"I know." Taylor cut her editor off with a heartfelt sigh of exasperation, figuring Jeremy had heard way too much already. Yet to turn off the speakerphone now would be to imply that she had something to hide. She didn't.

"There was someone a long time ago that I never dated and always had feelings for," Taylor continued in a low voice, avoiding Jeremy's steady appraising gaze, "but it wasn't Zak

Townsend. Believe me, he was not even on my radar when I was writing that novel. I barely knew who he was until he and Zoe approached me about buying the rights for *Sail Away*. Then, of course, I had to do a lot of research and get up to speed on their public personas before talking to them."

She had sensed—accurately, as it turned out—that Zak and Zoe Townsend's egos would not take kindly to any ignorance on her part, where their celebrity was concerned. So she had watched tapes of their reality TV show, read the articles about them in the legitimate magazines, and looked up the statistics on their newly formed production company. And naively bought into the myth that they were two nice, talented musicians/wannabe-actors who were genuinely in love with each other.

Jeremy walked into the adjacent laundry room, set up the ironing board and plugged in the iron. He rummaged through the cabinet until he found the can of spray starch.

Geraldine drummed her fingers on the other end of the connection. "We're going to have to combat this."

Taylor knew Geraldine's constant tapping was an indication of just how upset she was. That did not, however, mean she was prepared to fall into the trap that had been set for her. And she was sure now that she was the sacrificial lamb of the scandal.

"I'm not going to dignify such a ridiculous assertion with any action on my part," Taylor countered stubbornly while Jeremy, still listening implacably, began to iron his work clothes.

"You may want to rethink that, Taylor," Geraldine scolded, "because whoever leaked this information also sent the link to anchor Mandy Stone, on the *Short-takes TV* show, as well as the Cable News Channel, the *New York Daily Express* and the *Access L.A. TV* show. I've had calls from all of them, trying to confirm this, and they're clamoring for your phone number so they can talk directly to you."

Taylor rubbed at the tension building in her temples. "I'm not getting into a they-said-she-said public feud with Zak and Zoe. That would only keep the lies going."

"You may not have any choice," Geraldine warned. "This little tidbit just breathed new life into a scandal that was almost dead."

Finished ironing the first item, Jeremy shrugged out of his T-shirt and slipped into the starched light blue cotton. He left it unbuttoned, casually looped a striped tie around his neck and picked up his trousers.

Mouth dry at the sight of those well-toned abs, Taylor picked up her mug and walked over to take the glass carafe off the warmer. She directed her voice toward the phone, still on the table. "The question is, how did whoever leaked this information to that Web site know what my book was about? I've only let one person read it, and I know Paige would never have leaked anything to the tabloid press, never mind come to such a ridiculous conclusion about the hero." Unless..." Taylor paused, swallowed. Behind her, she heard the swish as Jeremy swept off his running shorts and put on his freshly pressed trousers. "Have you been sending out galleys?"

"No." Silence fell as Geraldine hesitated. "Except..."

Oh, no. "Who did you send it to?" Taylor demanded, dread welling up inside her.

Jeremy came to stand beside her, already buttoning up his shirt.

"A couple weeks ago, before all this gossip started, I had a call from Zak and Zoe's production company, and they wanted to know if you had anything else available for option. So I sent them a line-edited copy of *Mr. What If...?* to read." Geraldine drew a deep breath. "You don't think someone who works for Zak and Zoe would have done this. Do you?"

"Who knows?" Taylor said wearily, running a hand through

her hair. She was standing close enough to Jeremy to inhale the tantalizing fragrance of soap and aftershave lotion.

Lounging against the counter, he laced a comforting hand around her waist.

Taylor resisted the urge to bury her face in his chest, and just stay there until all the turmoil in her professional life subsided. She drew a stabilizing breath and bit her lip. "Zak and Zoe are not all that nice to the hired help, if you know what I mean. It's possible they have an enemy among their staff, who is feeding this story to the tabloids for money." It was also possible that Zak and Zoe were fanning the flames of this scandal deliberately. It had kept them in the news nearly every day for two weeks now.

Geraldine exhaled. "About the reporters who are trying to get in touch with you…"

"I'm not going to talk to them," Taylor repeated, even more firmly this time.

Jeremy lifted a brow, seeming to agree with Geraldine that Taylor's decision was the wrong one.

"Well, then, what do I tell them?" her editor demanded. "They're not going to stop calling here. It's a slow news week, in case you haven't noticed."

Since standing that close to Jeremy was making her want to kiss him, Taylor stepped away from him. She rubbed her fingers across her brow and concentrated on finishing her conversation. "Tell them the last time you talked to me I said something about getting in my Jeep and driving off to parts unknown. Something about camping in the wilds. Colorado. Idaho, maybe?" She was making this up as she went along.

"Are you thinking about doing that?" Geraldine asked, aghast.

Taylor closed her eyes and pressed her lips together resolutely. "If it's the only way to get any peace and put an end to this nonsense? You bet."

JEREMY WAITED, frustration building, until Taylor ended her conversation. Although it was clear she had been up for a while, working, she was still in her pajamas—pink and white striped low-slung cotton pants and a figure-hugging pink tank top. Her shiny black hair was swept up in a clip, her fair skin marred only by the blush staining her cheeks. "Tell me you're kidding about taking off," he said.

Looking every bit as stubborn as she was beautiful, she regarded him with mock innocence. "Shouldn't you be at work?"

Not the answer he'd been looking for. "My office hours don't start until nine o'clock this morning," he told her gruffly, wishing like hell she would stop putting her guard up and pushing him away. She was behaving as if she were hiding something. What, he didn't know. "It's seven-thirty." He inclined his head toward the digital clock on the microwave.

"Then why are you here?" She brushed past him, toward the laptop on the kitchen table. She sat down in front of it.

He sauntered closer. "I forgot I didn't have an iron—mine's in storage. I knew there was one here I could use. And I figured I could stop in and say hello to you, and make sure we were still on for tonight. Hey, you didn't answer my question." Facing her, he leaned over and flattened his hands on the table on either side of her. "*Were* you serious about running away again?"

Because if she was…

To his exasperation, Taylor's expression gave no clue what she was thinking or feeling. The silence strung out between them, more uncomfortable than ever. Finally, she shrugged. "I'm serious about putting an end to this harassment and all the stories about me. If sending reporters off on a wild goose chase accomplishes that…" She let her voice drift off. "Meantime," she turned her attention to the screen and clicked

Send on the e-mail containing her attached newspaper column, "I'm going to do a little sleuthing of my own."

Done, she shut off her computer and pushed back her chair. "And I'm going to start by paying a visit to the sheriff's station."

"Then I'll go with you," Jeremy said.

She held herself aloof, watching as he finished buttoning his shirt. "You don't have to do that."

"Sure I do," Jeremy countered amiably, "if I want us to be a team, and I do."

The question was, what did she want?

He was no longer sure.

DEPUTY RIO VASQUEZ WAS just sitting down at his desk in the sheriff's station when Taylor and Jeremy walked in. He smiled at them and gestured them over. "I was just about to call you-all."

"I was hoping you might have something more about the female paparazzo who's been stalking me."

"Actually, we do." Rio gestured for them to have a seat, as he filled them in. "Turns out the trespasser's real name is Matilda Recchi. She's an operative for the Galaxy Detective Agency in California. They specialize in following cheating spouses, uncovering fraud, tracking down celebrity stalkers and turning them over to the police."

Which meant what? Taylor wondered. Zoe had hired a detective to investigate Zak and Taylor, and the detective had decided to capitalize on what she discovered?

"Is Ms. Recchi responsible for all of the leaked stories and photographs of me and Jeremy and the Townsends?" she asked.

Rio nodded. "We were able to retrieve a laptop from the hotel room in San Angelo where she's been staying and because it was a stalking and trespassing charge we were able to get a search warrant for it. The e-mails, attachments and photo files show that she's been feeding these love-triangle stories to all the magazines and TV shows. There were twelve in all so far, dating back the last two weeks."

Taylor didn't know whether to be relieved or furious. In truth, she was a little of both. "Did you see anything about my new novel?"

Rio nodded. "That was the last e-mail sent before we arrested her for trespassing and stalking on Jeremy's ranch."

So Ms. Recchi had read the line-edited manuscript, too, or at least enough to know what it was about. How had she gotten hold of it? Taylor wondered. Had Ms. Recchi stolen it from Zak and Zoe's production office or from one of their employees? Taylor had never seen Zak read anything except the film script he had been shooting. That didn't mean an employee hadn't hand-carried it to him when he was working in Laramie. He could have just put it aside or left it lying around. Certainly, he was careless enough. Her new book meant nothing to him. Or a jealous Zoe could have dumped it in the trash. Matilda Recchi, already shadowing them, could have come along and retrieved it. Or Zoe could have given it to Matilda Recchi and asked her to create more of a scandal that would ultimately discredit Taylor. The possibilities were endless.

"Is my situation the only one Matilda Recchi is reporting on, or am I just the last in a long string of paparazzi targets?" Taylor asked.

"Everything else on the hard drive had to do with routine cases Matilda Recchi was looking into as a private detective. There were no other communications with tabloids or attempts to get any juicy gossip published. No blackmail or extortion attempts. So all we have on her is possession of a false ID card, trespassing and stalking. She has no criminal record, so as long as she ceases and desists her harassment of you and the Townsends—who by the way have told us they will not file a complaint, for fear of even further bad publicity—Ms. Recchi will plead guilty, pay a fine and that will be that. As long as she behaves herself in the future, of course."

"Which means it's not a fluke that Zak and I ended up being her target."

Rio stuck to the facts. "There's no record on her laptop of anyone employing or even encouraging her to do this. The detective agency that she works for back in Los Angeles denies she is on any sort of assignment for them. She told them she was taking two weeks comp time and vacation. The agency itself is reputable. We've confirmed that with the LAPD and we have no reason to think they'd be lying to us."

"What does Matilda Recchi have to say about all this?"

"Nothing." Rio grimaced. "She's not talking. Which, of course, is her right."

Taylor looked at Jeremy. He seemed to be thinking what she was. "Could we try?" she asked Rio.

"If she is willing to meet with you, I don't see why not," Rio replied. "Although you won't have long. Her attorney's in the process of posting bail right now."

They were shown into a small conference room. Several minutes later, Matilda Recchi walked in, dressed in a bright orange jumpsuit, and accompanied by a guard. Her usual heavy makeup was gone and her unstyled hair was pulled back in a careless ponytail. She sat down on the opposite side of the table, giving them a bored but wary look.

Hoping the experience of being locked up would make the woman more reasonable, Taylor dove right in. "I don't understand why you would want to destroy my reputation."

Matilda held up a hand. "Honey, it's nothing personal."

Taylor thought of all the lies that had been broadcast on

TV, smeared across the pages of magazines, and reported as gospel on the World Wide Web. Angry tears welled behind her eyes. "It is to me."

Matilda shrugged and continued looking apathetic. "You're a public person now," she explained. "That makes you fair game."

"For character assassination?" Jeremy put in, a warning glint in his eyes. He gave Taylor's hand a reassuring squeeze and waited for Matilda Recchi to continue.

She sat back in her chair, looking as tough as nails. "People want to know what it's like to work closely with a supercouple like Zak and Zoe. They want to know if Zak is fooling around with Ms. O'Quinn."

Resentment flared inside Taylor. Even if curiosity had started this, common decency should have ended it. "You were following me." She kept her voice as level as possible. "You have to know I wasn't messing around with Zak."

There was a brief flash of guilt, replaced by stone-cold determination, on Matilda Recchi's face.

Hoping she had a conscience somewhere, Taylor continued persuasively, "And you had no right to drag Jeremy into this, imply that I'm pregnant or any of those things about wanting to get married!"

"First of all," Matilda Recchi shot right back, "I just take the photos and state what it 'appears' to me is going on. People can draw their own conclusions. Secondly, the doc here is part of this." She paused to eye the way Jeremy was still holding Taylor's hand. "Because you're involved in this and he's involved with you, and I'm not making that up! You two were hot and heavy!"

Taylor flushed as the guard did his best to squelch a grin. She withdrew her hand from Jeremy's and stared Matilda Recchi down. "I want to know who is behind this. You didn't just start following me out of the blue. And I want to know how you leapt to the conclusion that my second novel is in any way, shape or form about Zak Townsend!"

"Give us that information and we'll do our best to see the local authorities go easy on you," Jeremy said.

Matilda Recchi smirked and sat back. "Give it up, both of you. Especially you, honey." She looked at Taylor. "You're way out of your league."

Matilda Recchi's lawyer walked in, in a thousand dollar suit. "We're done here," he said. He looked at Matilda, as if they were in cahoots and had been all along. "I paid your bail. You're free to go. The plane to Los Angeles is waiting."

MATILDA RECCHI'S PRIVATE JET transport back to L.A. via the Laramie airstrip was the talk of the town. By noon, everyone in Laramie seemed to know about it. By one o'clock, the first tabloid reporter arrived at the community hospital annex where the doctors' private practice offices were located, looking for Jeremy.

He managed to duck out without running into the guy and went to the newspaper office, where he had arranged to have a private lunch meeting with Brian Hilliard.

Brian ushered Jeremy into the conference room and shut the door. "Is Krista Sue all right?"

"That's what I wanted to talk to you about." Jeremy set two bags on the table. One carried their meal, which he had offered to bring, the other a little required reading for Brian. "Since the two of you are getting married in a few weeks, she gave me permission to keep you fully informed of any health issues that might come up for her."

"You're worried about those migraines she's been having, too?"

Jeremy did not try to hide his concern. "I think all her recent maladies are due to stress, a lot of which can be easily eliminated if you and Krista Sue are honest with each other."

Brian looked shocked, then upset at the idea he might be in any way responsible for his fiancée's migraines. "I haven't been keeping anything from her!"

That, Jeremy thought, was part of the problem. Brian was a little too vocal about his wishes where his wife-to-be was concerned. 'I can't tell you what's on Krista Sue's mind. Only she can do that. Before you ask her, I'd like you to read this."

"The Guy Who Sailed Away and the Girl Who Found Herself." Brian stared at the novel in his hands. "Why do you want me to read Taylor O'Quinn's first book?"

"Because hopefully it will do for you what it's already done for me and help you understand what twenty-something women want out of life." And it clearly wasn't what Brian had been giving Krista Sue.

Chapter Thirteen

Studio Execs Cancel Film

Citing examples of other failed attempts to turn pop-rockers into movie actors, Majestic Films International cancelled their contract with Zak and Zoe Townsend's Always Famous production company for the big-screen version of *Sail Away.* "There is simply no way this project can be fixed," the exec in charge said.

When asked to comment, Zak and Zoe Townsend agreed. "Looking back," Zoe Townsend claimed sadly, taking her husband's hand, " we can see that Ms. O'Quinn began sabotaging this project from the first moment she realized Zak was not interested in having a fling with her…"

Zak nodded. "It's been said 'hell hath no fury like a woman scorned'. This certainly seems to be the case, and we can only hope that Taylor O'Quinn will get the professional help she needs…"

Music Industry Daily newspaper, Los Angeles bureau
June 13

"Ms. O'Quinn? Would you like to comment?" the reporter asked Taylor again.

Wishing she'd had the foresight to screen her calls, Taylor sighed as she stared at the information that had just been e-mailed to her. A quick check showed her that a copy of the "breaking news" had already been posted to the *Music Industry Daily* newspaper Web site. It hadn't taken the reporter long to track her down after the press release went out about the film going belly up.

"When did you find out the movie had been cancelled?" The reporter continued pressing for a reaction from her.

"I haven't been told," Taylor said. She paused, not wanting to believe what she knew in her gut was probably accurate. "Are you sure this is true? *Sail Away* has been officially cancelled?" She didn't know whether to leap for joy or cry in disappointment. On the one hand, it would be great for her career if the mess Zak and Zoe had made of her story about the search for personal identity never saw the light of day. On the other hand, if the film didn't get distributed to theaters, or at least released on DVD, Zak and Zoe would not get paid and she would not get the rest of the money owed her, either. Which meant, she would remain broke as could be, and hence, once again deemed a failure in her family's eyes.

"Oh, yeah. The exec I talked to said he would have laughed his head off at the rough cut he saw if he hadn't been crying over all the money down the drain."

That at least sounded accurate, Taylor thought.

"So what do you have to say? Did you deliberately ruin the screenplay out of spite, as the Townsends have stated?"

What do you think? Taylor wanted to say. Why would I shoot myself in the foot? Knowing the worst thing she could do right now would be to talk off the cuff and keep this public feud going, Taylor stated in a deliberately pleasant tone, "I have no comment at this time."

"You're sure? I have to tell you—the Townsends have you looking pretty bad to the rest of the world with all they are asserting about you."

Misery engulfed her. Stronger than that was the desire to behave in a classy manner, foreign to the two pop-rockers. "I'll let you know if I change my mind," Taylor promised in the same even tone. "And thanks for the heads-up about the film cancellation." She hung up the phone.

Jeremy walked in. "More bad news?"

Taylor pointed to the computer screen.

"They just don't stop with the character assassination, do they?" he said grimly after reading the tabloid report.

Taylor shrugged and tried not to look as defeated as she felt. "They have to blame someone for the colossal failure. It's sure as heck not going to be them." She was the likely target, unfair as it was.

"Obviously, you're fighting back," Jeremy surmised.

And make herself look as petty and vengeful as the two of them? No way. "This will stay in the news for two to three days, at most," Taylor assured him.

"The damage to your reputation will be permanent," he warned.

Would it? And even if it were…

She stood and pushed back her chair. "I don't want to talk about it any more right now."

His gaze softened. He seemed to know intuitively she needed time to absorb this latest turn of events before she could figure out what to do next.

He clapped a companionable arm about her waist and pulled her close. "We still on for dinner this evening?"

Taylor's anxiety subsided at the feel of his warmth and

strength. It didn't matter how bad her life got—he always made her feel better. "Absolutely." She smiled, brightening at the thought. "But I'd like to meet you at your office."

His eyes darkened seductively. "Any particular reason you don't want me to pick you up?"

"I've got an appointment to have my Jeep serviced this afternoon, at the garage in town. It's not going to be ready until six-thirty. Since I'll already be in town, it makes sense for me not to go all the way back out to the ranch just so you can drive out, pick me up and bring me back to town again." He could still drive her to dinner. They'd just leave her Liberty in the hospital parking lot.

He let her go, stepped back. "I didn't know you were having a problem with your SUV," he said.

"It's just routine maintenance. The kind of stuff you get done before—or after—any long trip. I should have had it done before I left California." She moved on to a more important topic. "So what's this I hear about you giving out my first novel to Brian Hilliard as required reading?"

Since she'd returned to Texas, Taylor noted approvingly, Jeremy'd gone a long way from disapproving of her writing career, to being a major cheerleader. She couldn't help but be happy about that. His complete support of her profession made up for all the skeptics she still had in her life.

A sheepish grin tugged at the corners of his lips. "How'd you know about that?" He rubbed the flat of his palm across the back of his neck.

"I saw the copy of it on Brian's desk. He told me what you said when you dropped by to see him this afternoon." Unable to resist teasing Jeremy a little, she asked, "So what gives? You channeling Dr. Phil all of a sudden?" He had never seemed like the kind of guy who would offer relationship advice. To anyone.

He held up a hand in entreat. "There's a fine line between

interfering and helping. I know that. But given the number of stress-related illnesses Krista Sue's had in the past few months, I would be remiss if I didn't have a man to man talk with Brian, both as their physician, and their friend. That's what family medicine is all about—treating the whole family."

"So you told him to read my novel?"

Jeremy shrugged. "I saw a lot of myself and the mistakes I've made in the hero in your book, and I think they're the same mistakes a lot of guys in their twenties make at some point. I lost a chance to be with a woman because I wouldn't see what she really needed in life, and she didn't have confidence that she could talk openly with me."

"Are we talking about your ex now?" she asked softly.

He shook his head and took her hands in his. "We're talking about you."

Taylor stared at Jeremy, her heart pounding.

He tightened his grip on her hands and went on, "I fell for you the first day we met."

Shock warred with the joy she felt. "You never let on…."

He shook his head, his regret about that obvious. He slipped an arm about her waist and brought her closer, the nearness of him and the intimacy of the moment filling her senses. "I knew we could be great friends and the beginning of med school was—" He paused as if searching for the right word.

"Overwhelming?" Taylor guessed, breathing in the masculine fragrance of his hair and skin.

"To say the least." He met her gaze. "Only a fool would have picked that time to start a romantic relationship and expect it to last."

"And then I disappointed you by dropping out of med school," Taylor recollected sadly.

He quirked his brow. "At the time I thought I was angry because you were wasting your talent, and the opportunity to become a doctor." His eyes darkened to a deeper brown. "Looking back, I think I just didn't want you to leave me."

Taylor hadn't wanted to leave him, either. In fact, had he supported her choices more, she probably would have stayed in Texas and launched her writing career there. Knowing Jeremy was so opposed to her career shift, however, had motivated her to start a new life on a different coast. Ultimately, she had run from the pain. Run from him.

Jeremy's hold on her gentled. "I made too many judgments, based on what I assumed was going on with you. I never gave you a chance to tell me what was really on your mind, and I didn't listen to what you did manage to say."

Taylor tightened her grip on him in return. "You had every right to doubt me, considering how many times I've run away from my problems. I should have explained. Helped you understand where I was coming from. If I had, we wouldn't have broken up."

"Instead, we would have found a way to face our problems together," he murmured as his lips descended ever so slowly and surely to hers. His kiss was hotter and sweeter than she expected and left her feeling ravished and wanted and utterly sure he was the man she was supposed to spend the rest of her life with.

Lifting her arms, she wreathed them around his neck and kissed him back deeply, over and over, until all the layers of restraint fell away. She felt his need as surely as her own. They drew back contentedly, knowing the rest would have to wait for later this evening.

Exhaling, he surveyed her from head to toe. His eyes glittered with ardor. "Damn, Taylor…"

A silence fell between them. Taylor drew a breath, unsure if this was the time to tell him everything else. The only thing she knew for certain was that she never wanted her time with him to end.

"So about tonight?" he said, misunderstanding the reason behind her momentary confusion.

Taylor smiled. There was no need to rush. What was in her heart could wait for a more intimate setting. She rose on tiptoe and brushed her lips across his jaw in a fleeting gesture of goodbye. "I'll meet you at your office at six-thirty," she said.

"Ms. O'QUINN!" the reporter shouted outside Laramie Community Hospital. "We didn't expect to find you here!"

"Your editor said you were off to the Rockies!" shouted another.

A third shoved a microphone in Taylor's face. "Care to tell us how you feel about Zak and Zoe Townsend's assertion you deliberately wrecked their movie?"

"All right. That's enough. Back up!" Deputy Rio Vasquez barked, stepping out of his patrol car and into the center of the noisy fray. "We told you an hour ago to stay away from the entrance to the hospital."

Rio escorted Taylor through the automatic glass doors and kept the throng of reporters from following.

Taylor hurried through the lobby. People were staring. She couldn't blame them. A scandal of this magnitude had never swept through Laramie before. Now it had and was all due to her…and Zak and Zoe.

Face burning with embarrassment, she stepped into the elevator and headed to the third floor. From there, she rushed toward the elevated breezeway that would take her to the annex where Jeremy's office was located.

Six-forty; it was blissfully quiet.

Hurriedly, she stepped through the door that said Jeremy Carrigan, M.D. He was waiting for her. "I'm so sorry I'm late."

"You got caught by the reporters, didn't you?" He wrapped

her in a welcoming embrace that felt as warm and strong as he did.

She nodded, resting her head against his muscled chest. "Please tell me they haven't been bothering you."

He let out an exasperated breath. "Hospital security had to be called three times this afternoon. I left half a dozen messages on your cell."

She closed her eyes. "My battery ran out. I haven't had a chance to recharge it."

Jeremy drew back. He stepped around behind her to massage the tense muscles in her back and shoulders. "Where've you been?"

She let her head fall back as she succumbed to the blissful kneading of his palms. "The public library." His touch felt so good it was all she could do not to melt in a puddle on the floor. "Since I had to wait for my SUV, I decided to use the time to research my next novel."

He came around in front of her. "You've started it?"

"I have a rough idea what I want to write about." She looked past him and out the window. "They're still across the street." Amazingly, the mob of paparazzi seemed to be growing.

Jeremy grimaced. "I'm sure it won't be long before they try to sneak back in again."

Behind them, the door opened. Luke and Meg walked into their son's office suite. Meg was in nurses' scrubs, Luke a shirt, tie and white physician's jacket. Both were still wearing their LCH staff badges.

"You heard," Jeremy guessed with a frown.

Luke Carrigan nodded. He did not look pleased.

Visibly upset, Meg Carrigan added, "They've been trying to get quotes from us, too. They're even interviewing people as they leave the hospital to see if they know anything about this 'situation' you're in."

"I'm so sorry," Taylor said again, feeling all the more embarrassed.

"Which is why we wanted to talk to you," Luke told Jeremy in a flat, no nonsense tone. "We think it's time you took a vacation."

FIVE MINUTES LATER, the door shut behind Luke and Meg. Taylor and Jeremy were alone once again. "Well. It's not every day a guy gets an enforced vacation," Jeremy said, making light of the dressing down he had just gotten for bringing chaos to the community medical center.

Taylor looked as ticked off as he felt. "This would not have happened if not for me," she seethed, crossing her arms militantly in front of her.

"You didn't have anything to do with it," he reminded her, starting toward her. "Zak and Zoe Townsend created this mess."

"Even so…" Taylor stopped, shook her head grimly. "I can't go out with you tonight."

Taking heed of her defiant posture, Jeremy stayed where he was. "Because of the reporters? We can ditch them and still go on our date."

She made a face. "I have something to do."

That sounded mysterious. Unfortunately, she showed no signs of enlightening him.

Not appreciating being shut out at this stage of the game, he prodded, "Or somewhere to go?"

Taylor's expression became closed. "The less you know the better."

Jeremy stood, legs braced apart, hands on his waist. "This has an unpleasant ring."

She began to pace. "I can't involve you in my problem any more."

He resisted the urge to take her in his arms and kiss some

sense into her, only because he knew it was the gentlemanly thing to do. "It's my mess, too."

"Exactly." She whirled to face him, her silky black hair swirling about the slender shoulders bared by her form-fitting summer dress. "But not for much longer."

He set his jaw, too. "I don't want you going off alone," he repeated.

She looked him in the eye. "I know."

"But it doesn't change your mind," he guessed, temper sparking.

She released a short breath. "No," she said quietly. "It doesn't."

Suddenly, it all made sense. Jeremy knew why she was so calm. This was no spur-of-the-moment decision. It was a well-thought-out strategy that she had not cared to advise him about. "That's why you wanted your Jeep all ready for a road trip, isn't it?" He strode close. "You knew you were going to leave again."

"I knew I might have to," Taylor corrected.

He cupped her shoulders, persuaded gently, "Then let me go with you. I've got two weeks off."

She extricated herself from his light, staying grasp. "I can't hurt you any more than I already have, by putting you in the middle of this public relations nightmare."

"So you're just going to run away?" he asked in disbelief.

She shook her head at his concern. "I'll be back in a few days."

"That's what you said the last time you took off for parts unknown." Same car, nearly same scenario. Same heartache. Only worse this time. Much worse.

She appeared to be holding herself together with effort. It was little comfort, given what she was talking about doing.

"It won't be seven years this time." She offered what consolation she could.

He wasn't buying it.

"I know what I'm doing, Jeremy," she continued, begin-ning to get as upset with him as he was with her. "You've got to believe me. *This is for the best*."

If only he could believe that. But he knew Taylor, knew that when the chips were down, when she felt overwhelmed, she got in the car and took off. And in the process left every-thing—and everyone—that had been upsetting her far behind. He'd thought that was all behind them, but apparently not.

He wasn't going to let her pretend this was anything else but that same escape strategy, all over again. "Now you really sound like you're breaking up with me," he told her dryly.

She flinched. Her cool determination returned. "I don't want to break up with you," she retorted emotionally, holding his gaze, "but you have to trust that I know what I'm doing because I *can't* be with someone who won't let me be me. Whether they understand or approve or not!"

Jeremy had stood by and let her get away with this before. Not again. Not ever again. Whether she liked it or not, he was going to make her face what she was doing. What she did after that was her choice. "And I can't be with someone who walks out on me and runs away every time the going gets rough," he told her, just as firmly. "If you leave here without telling me precisely where you're going, and what you're going to do, and when you'll be back, then…" Hardly able to believe it had come to this, he let his voice trail off.

She studied him for a long moment, the air fraught with emotion. "We're done?"

Figuring it was time to lay all their cards on the table, he let his disappointment show. "Yes."

She gave him another long look, one that let him know she felt deeply hurt and disillusioned, too. Then without another word, she walked out the door…and out of his life.

As it turned out, Taylor only drove as far as the DFW airport. While waiting for her flight to Los Angeles, she purchased a one day pass to the Captain's Club on her credit card and made the first of ten very important calls.

By the time she landed at LAX, a television crew was waiting for her. A bungalow at a posh Beverly Hills hotel, frequented by privacy-seeking celebrities, had been rented and prepared. All Taylor had to do was show up and put her plan in motion.

She made two more phone calls. And then waited. In less than an hour, she was well on her way to clearing her name.

"I guess you heard the studio canceled *Sail Away*," Zak Townsend said as soon as he strolled in, his wife by his side. Dressed in designer clothing, they looked as glamorous as ever.

"Contrary to what you've been saying in the press, though, it wasn't due to me," Taylor said struggling to control her temper.

"We agree." Zoe perched on the sofa, crossed her legs and cupped her palms around her knee. "We thought the new stuff you wrote was terrific and we plan to use the footage shot by our production company in our upcoming music videos."

"Then I should get paid."

"Technically, I don't think we have to do that." Zach went straight to the suite bar and helped himself to a shot of tequila. "Since the movie isn't being made—but I guess you've earned it."

"I also want to set the record straight," Taylor continued, staring straight at him. "By going on Mandy Stone's show and letting everyone know you and I did not have an affair."

Zoe leapt up from the sofa. She marched toward Taylor, waving her arms. "We can't let you do that!" she said. "That would make me look nutty!"

"As opposed to making me look like an immoral slut?" Taylor shot right back. She marched forward to face off with Zoe. "We all know I never slept with Zak. Never had any interest in him. Didn't base a book on a crush about him. And I certainly didn't try to break up your marriage or set out to deliberately ruin your first feature film, by producing a bad script!"

Zoe looked bored. She went to the mirror to check her hair. "What's your point?" she said, over her shoulder.

Taylor set her jaw. "My point is that the two of you have been spreading lies about me. And you used a private detective to follow me to Texas, snap the photos and feed the stories to the tabloids."

Zak scoffed and poured himself another shot of tequila. "Matilda Recchi never said that."

"Funny," Taylor responded, with the kind of über sophisticated cool she didn't know she had, "I don't recall mentioning the private detective's name."

"Well, I…we…he…" Zoe stammered, casting a panicked look at her husband.

"We must have heard it on the news," Zak muttered.

Zoe nodded quickly in agreement.

"It hasn't been on the news," Taylor replied, watching the two pop-rockers blanch all the more. Deciding to go for broke, she bluffed her way through the rest, announcing what she deduced had happened behind the scenes of the well-orchestrated scandal that had left her in the ditch and Zak and Zoe blameless. "Which you know very well," Taylor continued, "because as soon as Ms. Recchi got word to you that she had been arrested for trespassing and stalking, you sent a fancy lawyer to bail her out of jail in Texas and put her on a private jet back to California. What you may not know, is that her laptop computer was confiscated by the Laramie sheriff's department before all that happened, and they have all the proof I need to demonstrate that the two of you were behind the attempts to wreck my professional and personal reputation."

Zoe glared at Taylor. "I hope you're not thinking of suing us for defamation."

Taylor held her ground. "Why shouldn't I?"

Zak's expression turned threatening. "Because we'll deny it and it will get ugly."

"Try being grateful for a change," Zoe interjected sweetly, laying her hand on her husband's arm as she faced Taylor once again. "Before all this started, Taylor honey, no one even knew who you were. We made you famous."

As if that were some kind of manna from heaven. "And the damage to my public persona?" Taylor returned, curious as to what they thought about that.

Zak shrugged. "Nothing a little 'professionally prescribed R & R' wouldn't cure."

"Or well-timed piece of videotape." It was Taylor's turn to smile. She walked to the adjacent bedroom, opened the door, and looked at the film crew who had been discreetly recording everything for the most popular tabloid TV show in the country.

"You-all got that?" Taylor asked smugly, feeling triumphant at long last, while Zak and Zoe gasped in horror behind her. "Or do you need us to do it again?"

Chapter Fourteen

Zak and Zoe Expect To Rebound From Crisis

Zak and Zoe Townsend have checked in to the Enlightenment Rehabilitation Center in Malibu, California, seeking treatment for their interpersonal relationship dysfunction. They are expected to stay for thirty days and had no statement for the press. Upon their release, they will be sitting for an exclusive interview with this publication.

Personalities! magazine
June 14

"I would have thought you would be happier," Geraldine Meyerson told Taylor.

In Dallas for a writers' conference, Geraldine had asked Taylor to meet her for a business lunch. Just off the plane from her impromptu trip to California, in no real hurry to return to Laramie for her things, Taylor had agreed.

"You cleared your name," Taylor's editor continued, visibly pleased. "People are clamoring to read both your novels. Hence, orders from bookstores are through the roof. We've moved publication of both books up substantially to capitalize on the demand and greatly expanded the advertising budget for your books." She beamed as she sipped her iced tea. "You're now an A-list author at our publishing house and thanks to diligent work from our P.R. department, you have two solid weeks of interviews and appearances lined up, starting next week. So why the frown? Does it have anything to do with that hunky doctor back in Laramie?"

Taylor ran her fork through her salad, aware she hadn't ever felt this dejected and depressed. "We broke it off."

Geraldine studied her, with the wisdom of a fifty-something woman who had it all—career, husband, kids. "That doesn't mean your feelings vanished. I'd figure you would know that better than anyone."

Taylor did. But there were times, when loving someone and having them love you back just wasn't enough. "He didn't trust that I could handle Zak and Zoe myself." He'd thought she was running away again. And she wasn't sure she could forgive Jeremy for that. Taylor sat up straighter. She forced herself to take a bite of her lunch, even though she was so upset it was all she could do to swallow. "I need people who believe in me in my life."

People who stood by her no matter what.

"You also need the give and take of a healthy adult relationship." Geraldine gave Taylor a long, intent look, then said gently but firmly, "Take it from someone who's been married a long time, Taylor. There are going to be times you disagree with the man in your life. Times when you just can't come to terms with each other. That's when you let each other do your own thing, stand or fail on your own, and at the end of the day, still love and respect each other."

Taylor ignored the ache in her throat that usually presaged tears. "You make it sound so easy."

"It isn't." Geraldine regarded her soberly. "But when you really love someone, you find a way to be there for each other without trying to stifle each other's growth or setting a lot of 'either or' terms and conditions. And you do it because life with that person is so much better than life without."

"HEY, DR. CARRIGAN," Krista Sue Wright waved from the other end of the passageway, outside his office door. "I'm glad I caught you."

Jeremy waited for her to catch up.

"I heard you were going to be taking a couple of weeks off," Krista Sue continued breathlessly, "but then…you didn't…after all…"

Only because the paparazzi dogging him had dispersed, and gone off to chase yet another breaking story. And it was all thanks to Taylor's savvy actions out in California. Jeremy had seen the footage of the confrontation on the *Short-takes!* tabloid TV show, along with everyone else in Laramie. So instead of being off on a two-week enforced vacation, he had remained in Laramie, seeing patients, and taking shifts as the on call family physician in the hospital E.R. When he hadn't been practicing medicine, he'd been working on his ranch, thinking about Taylor and how it had all gone wrong.

He turned his attention to the patient who'd had way too many ailments and injuries over the course of the last six weeks. "You're looking healthy." For a change…

"I feel good." Wicker basket and wrapped present in hand, Krista Sue smiled and leaned against the corridor wall as he finished locking up. "And it's all because of you," she continued effusively. "And the novel Taylor wrote that you made Brian read. He came to me when he finished it. We had a long heart-to-heart talk and worked out a solution. I'm going to honor the contract I signed with the school district, teach for one year, and give it my all. Because Brian's right, I've wanted to be a teacher all my life, and I owe it to myself to give it a shot. And I'm also going to do an unpaid sewing apprenticeship with Jenna Lockhart Designs every Saturday for one year. Because I really love sewing, too. Then we'll see which career I like best and would like to pursue."

Jeremy smiled. "That sounds like a good compromise."

"It is." Krista Sue laid her hand over her heart. "I feel so much better already. Thank you for talking to Brian and making me deal with all the stuff that had been bothering me."

"You're welcome." There was nothing Jeremy liked better than helping one of his patients feel better.

"Anyway, this is from me and Brian." She gave him the gift basket filled with ripe Texas peaches. "And this is for Taylor." She handed over the wrapped present, as well. "We didn't know how to get in touch with her. It's a framed copy of her first column for the newspaper. We thought she might like to have it. I tried calling her cell phone, but all I've been able to do was get her voice mail. So I figured you would know how to get it to her, since of course you'll be seeing her sooner than we will."

Would he? Jeremy wondered. Taylor had been absent from his life for three days now. It felt like three years. The weekend loomed ahead of him like a long empty abyss.

"I'll do my best to see she gets it," Jeremy promised.

"Great. And thanks again! And by the way, we're inviting you both to our wedding!" Krista Sue bounded off, happy as can be.

Jeremy took the stairs down to the floor beneath where Paige's office suite was located. Like him, she was just locking up for the day.

"Jeremy! Just the person I'm looking for! I have something for you," Paige said, reaching into her canvas carryall.

Hope rose within him, even as he braced himself for further

disappointment. What he wanted was a message, a sign, anything that would indicate Taylor was as sorry about the way things had ended between them as he. "Have you heard from Taylor?"

"Whether I have or haven't I can't tell you. I promised her I wouldn't say." With a rueful look in his direction, Paige pressed a thick manila envelope into his hand.

Jeremy's spirits fell. Obviously, he had let Taylor down one time too many. She was not going to forgive him. And for that, he could hardly blame her. She had wanted him to believe in her as fiercely as she believed in herself and trust that she could handle the situation by herself. Instead, he'd feared she was running away from trouble, the way she had in the past. His ultimatum had backfired, with Taylor obviously preferring to end their relationship and weather the battle alone rather than endure his lack of faith in her one second longer.

He passed Paige the wrapped present, explaining, "This is for Taylor. It's from Krista Sue Wright and Brian Hilliard."

Paige promptly returned it to him. "Give it to Taylor yourself."

"I don't think she wants to see me."

"Question is," Paige arched her brow, "do you want to see her?"

Hell, yes. He hadn't known it was possible to miss her so much. "She made it pretty clear she didn't want my help or presence in her life. I'm not interested in getting involved with a woman whose desire for me is a short-term thing."

Paige did a double take. "You think Taylor was just with you because you were both here? Because it was…convenient?"

It hadn't seemed like a casual fling at the time. Hindsight seemed to indicate different. Jeremy shrugged, refusing to let Paige make him feel stupid. "Seems clear enough. She hasn't called or come back, has she?"

Paige scoffed. "Have you called her?"

He'd been waiting for Taylor to come back to Laramie first. And had she really wanted to make up with him that probably would have happened two days ago. "I wanted to do it in person."

"Uh-huh." Paige inclined her head at the heavy manila envelope, looking wiser than he could ever hope to be. "Well, rancher, before you do anything else foolhardy, you might want to read that."

TAYLOR DROVE OUT to the Chamberlain ranch, arriving late Friday night. Early Saturday morning, while Paige was still sleeping in, she showered and dressed and began packing up her things. She nearly had her Jeep loaded when a familiar pickup truck turned into the drive.

Jeremy parked beside her Jeep and got out. Damn, if he didn't look good in a pair of jeans and a western cut long-sleeved white shirt. His auburn hair was damp and rumpled, his jaw closely shaven. He smelled of soap and cologne and the essence that was uniquely him. Her pulse raced as he neared her. "Going somewhere?" he asked in a husky voice that sent shivers across her skin.

Doing her best to hold her spiraling emotions in check, Taylor forced herself to meet his gaze. "As a matter of fact, yes."

His lips took on a contemplative slant. "Planning to say goodbye?" he continued, a questioning look in his brown eyes.

"To you? No. At least—" Taylor paused and bit her lip, wondering if the same thing that was on her mind was on his "—I hoped I wouldn't have to."

Nodding, he pressed his thumbs through the belt loops on either side of his fly and rocked forward on his toes. His expression grew all the more serious. "I have something to say. If you still want to go after that, I won't stop you."

Taylor waited, her heart hammering in her chest. She

rocked forward on her toes, too, and looked up into his face. Suddenly, she wanted this to work out, so much....

He looked at her in such a way, she knew whatever he was about to say was coming straight from his heart. "I was wrong not to believe you could handle Zak and Zoe," he stated in a voice thick with emotion. "You did an amazing job with that."

Taylor's throat closed up a little, too. "Thank you," she whispered, happiness and relief welling inside her.

He continued looking deep into her eyes. "I should have trusted that you would know what to do."

Taylor drew a breath, knowing just how important it was they get this clear. "Yes. You should have," she said quietly, knowing he wasn't the only one at fault here. "And I should have let you stand with me. Because the minute they dragged you into it, by putting your face and name in the tabloids, it became your fight, too."

Jeremy held up a hand, letting her know he wasn't finished. "The point is, they're in rehab. And that fight is over." A slow smile spread across his face. Tenderness filled his voice. "And an even more important one is about to begin." He wrapped an arm about her waist, and guided her close. "Especially now that I know that our affair wasn't a momentary impulse on your part."

Taylor began to flush. She studied his teasing expression...and knew. "You read the galleys for *Mr. What If...?*, didn't you?"

He chuckled. A slight inclination of his handsome head indicated this was so. He tucked her hair behind her ear. "Are you ever going to get tired of writing about me?"

"*Mr. What If...?* was my attempt to put you out of my heart and my mind."

"By writing about what it would be like if we ever did get together?" he murmured, pleased.

Trying not to be too embarrassed Taylor whispered, "Yes."

He covered her lips with his and kissed her tenderly. "And how did your fantasy compare to the real thing?"

She reveled in his warm embrace. "Couldn't hold a candle."

He smiled. "My feelings exactly."

Another kiss, deeper and more intimate this time.

When at last they drew apart just enough to take a breath, he said, "I love you, Taylor. I'm sorry I hurt you and didn't stand by you, but if you're willing to give me another chance…."

It was Taylor's turn to chuckle. "Where do you think I was going just now?" she asked.

His gaze grew speculative. "To see me—at Lago Vista Ranch."

Epilogue

Best-Selling Author To Wed

On the eve of the publication of her unabashedly sentimental and riotously funny third novel, *Home to Love*,
writer Taylor O'Quinn will marry local family physician
and gentleman rancher, Jeremy Carrigan. When asked
to comment on the last year of their life, the happy
couple said, "It doesn't get any better than this…"

June 15, one year later
The Laramie Press

The Lago Vista Ranch house gleamed in the late afternoon
sunshine. Much had changed in the twelve months since
Jeremy had officially taken up residence on the lake-view
property. He'd hired an architect to add two more bedrooms
with adjoining baths, a writing studio for Taylor, a study for
him. The central living area had been expanded, a welcoming front porch, and lagoon style swimming pool, similar to
the one in which he and Taylor had first met up again in,
added. The exterior of the now-hexagonal-shaped abode had
been painted a creamy white, a red tile roof added. Beautiful

landscaping, designed and implemented by Jeremy's sister Susie, surrounded the inviting dwelling.

At sunset, guests would arrive, and they'd all head for the hill above the water, where folding chairs and a flower-draped arbor had already been set up. But for now, having decided the precious hours before their wedding were better spent together than—as tradition usually dictated—apart, Taylor and Jeremy relaxed poolside, with a glass of wine, delaying the moment they'd have to part to dress for the festivities ahead.

A FedEx courier walked around the side of the house. "Package for you, Ms. O'Quinn." He handed over an electronic pen and pad for signature.

Taylor complied, then accepted the mailing box addressed to her.

"What is it?" Jeremy asked, after the courier strode off.

Taylor opened it, and spying the contents, couldn't help but laugh. She removed the thick tome from the box and handed over a hardcover tell-all bearing Zak and Zoe's photos and names.

"Introspection—The Journey Back From Rehab," Jeremy read the lettering on the dust jacket.

Taylor removed the rest of the gift. "They also sent autographed copies of their brand new CDs—which are both dedicated to me 'for showing them the way'—and a personal note thanking me for my part in their newfound success."

Jeremy chuckled and shook his head. "Ironic, isn't it?"

"That they've turned their antics from a negative to a positive, and their company, Always Famous, from a failed movie development venture into an enormously successful music video-producing business? And along the way become bigger than ever? Although, for that matter," Taylor mused, recollecting all the changes the last year had wrought for her professionally, "so am I." She not only had success as a novelist now, she had a weekly column that was being syndicated in two dozen newspapers. Not bad, for a writer who was still just getting started. "I would never have believed it at the time, but the whole mess gave me real name recognition."

"And the contents of your books—your incredible ability to tell a love story and write about the life of the twenty and thirty-something woman—kept it going."

In the last year her novels had appeared on multiple bestseller lists. She'd even received more movie option and screenwriting and music-video scripting offers, all of which she had promptly turned down. From now on, she was only going to write about the subjects that interested her and spin the yarns she wanted to spin.

"My only question is," Jeremy taunted, pulling her over onto his lap, "What are you going to do when you run out of things to write about us?" He nuzzled the sensitive skin behind her ear.

Unable to deny he'd provided powerful inspiration for her work, Taylor put her glass aside and wrapped her arms about his neck. She lifted her lips to his. "The day will never come when you stop inspiring me."

He bent his head and kissed her. Holding her close, he whispered, "Have I told you I love you today?"

Taylor cuddled close, adoring his warmth and strength. "Only about a dozen times. And I love you, too."

He threaded his fingers through her hair and kissed her again, even more deeply and reverently this time. "I'm very glad you're going to be my wife."

Taylor smiled. "And I'm glad you're going to be my husband, too."

Five hours later, hearts brimming with joy, the two of them walked hand-in-hand up the hillside overlooking the lake, where guests were gathered. With family and friends surrounding them, they promised to love and cherish each other from this day forward. By the time the minister pronounced them husband and wife, the sun was descending in the western sky.

The wedding party made their way back to the ranch house, where caterers had set up an amazing spread.

"We're so happy and so proud of you," Taylor's parents said.

Taylor hugged them both.

Beaming, Jeremy embraced them, too.

Group by lively group, the siblings and offspring from each side of the family added their congratulations, too. "Can you believe it?" Meg Carrigan asked her husband Luke as the band began to play. "All four of our children are married!" Her sweeping glance took in Rebecca and Trevor clutching their twin toddlers' tiny hands, Susie and Tyler doting on their baby daughter, and Teddy and Amy standing proudly with their infant son. "Three of them have become parents!"

Taylor and Jeremy both knew how much that meant to his folks. To the Carrigans, family was everything.

"Soon you'll be able to make that four," Jeremy promised with a wink as the waiters passed out a round of champagne and sparkling cider. He wrapped his arm around Taylor's waist. "Because if Taylor and I have our way, we'll begin our own family very soon." They were already discussing names and the color of the nursery.

And nine months later, to the day…

Local Baby Boom Continues!

Jeremy Carrigan and Taylor-O'Quinn Carrigan welcomed triplet daughters to the world at Laramie Community Hospital, Saturday afternoon. Megan,

Melinda and Madeline are all doing well and expected to go home very soon...

The Laramie Community Hospital Newsletter
March 16

* * * * *

Nate Dempsey has returned to Whitehorse to uncover the truth about his past...

Nate sensed someone watching the house and looked out in surprise to see a woman astride a paint horse just on the other side of the fence. He quickly stepped back from the filthy second-floor window, although he doubted she could have seen him. Only a little of the June sun pierced the dirty glass to glow on the dust-coated floor at his feet as he waited a few heartbeats before he looked out again.

The place was so isolated he hadn't expected to see another soul. Like the front yard, the dirt road was waist-high with weeds. When he'd broken the lock on the back door, he'd had to kick aside a pile of rotten leaves that had blown in from last fall.

As he sneaked a look, he saw that she was still there, staring at the house in a way that unnerved him. He shielded his eyes from the glare of the sun off the dirty window and studied her, taking in her head of long blond hair that feathered out in the breeze from under her Western straw hat.

She wore a tan canvas jacket, jeans and boots. But it was

the way she sat astride the brown-and-white horse that nudged the memory.

He felt a chill as he realized he'd seen her before. In that very spot. She'd been just a kid then. A kid on a pretty paint horse. Not this one—the markings were different. Anyway, it couldn't have been the same horse, considering the last time he had seen her was more than twenty years ago. That horse would be dead by now.

His mind argued it probably wasn't even the same girl. But he knew better. It was the way she sat the horse, so at home in a saddle and secure in her world on the other side of that fence.

To the boy he'd been, she and her horse had represented freedom, a freedom he'd known he would never have—even after he escaped this house.

Nate saw her shift in the saddle, and for a moment he feared she planned to dismount and come toward the house. With Ellis Harper in his grave, there would be little to keep her away.

To his relief, she reined her horse around and rode back the way she'd come.

As he watched her ride away, he thought about the way she'd stared at the house—today and years ago. While the smartest thing she could do was to stay clear of this house, he had a feeling she'd be back.

Finding out her name should prove easy, since he figured she must live close by. As for her interest in Harper House… He would just have to make sure it didn't become a problem.

* * * * *

Be sure to look for
MATCHMAKING WITH A MISSION
and other suspenseful Harlequin Intrigue stories,
available in April
wherever books are sold.

INTRIGUE

WHITEHORSE MONTANA

No matter how much Nate Dempsey's past haunted
him, McKenna Bailey couldn't keep him off her mind.
He'd returned to town to bury his troubled youth—
but she wouldn't stop pursuing him until he was
working on the ranch by her side.

Look for

MATCHMAKING WITH A MISSION

BY

B.J. DANIELS

*Available in April
wherever books are sold.*

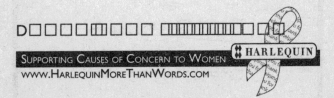

REQUEST YOUR FREE BOOKS!
2 FREE NOVELS PLUS 2
FREE GIFTS!

American ★ Romance®

Heart, Home & Happiness!

YES! Please send me 2 FREE Harlequin American Romance® novels and my 2 FREE gifts (gifts are worth about $10). After receiving them, if I don't wish to receive any more books, I can return the shipping statement marked "cancel." If I don't cancel, I will receive 4 brand-new novels every month and be billed just $4.24 per book in the U.S. or $4.99 per book in Canada, plus 25¢ shipping and handling per book and applicable taxes, if any*. That's a savings of close to 15% off the cover price! I understand that accepting the 2 free books and gifts places me under no obligation to buy anything. I can always return a shipment and cancel at any time. Even if I never buy another book from Harlequin, the two free books and gifts are mine to keep forever.   154 HDN EEZK 354 HDN EEZV

Name _____ (PLEASE PRINT) _____

Address _____ Apt. # _____

City _____ State/Prov. _____ Zip/Postal Code _____

Signature (if under 18, a parent or guardian must sign)

Mail to the **Harlequin Reader Service**:
IN U.S.A.: P.O. Box 1867, Buffalo, NY 14240-1867
IN CANADA: P.O. Box 609, Fort Erie, Ontario L2A 5X3

Not valid to current subscribers of Harlequin American Romance books.

Want to try two free books from another line?
Call 1-800-873-8635 or visit www.morefreebooks.com.

* Terms and prices subject to change without notice. N.Y. residents add applicable sales tax. Canadian residents will be charged applicable provincial taxes and GST. This offer is limited to one order per household. All orders subject to approval. Credit or debit balances in a customer's account(s) may be offset by any other outstanding balance owed by or to the customer. Please allow 4 to 6 weeks for delivery. Offer available while quantities last.

Your Privacy: Harlequin is committed to protecting your privacy. Our Privacy Policy is available online at www.eHarlequin.com or upon request from the Reader Service. From time to time we make our lists of customers available to reputable third parties who may have a product or service of interest to you. If you would prefer we not share your name and address, please check here. ☐

Romantic SUSPENSE

Sparked by Danger, Fueled by Passion.

The Taken

Tierney Doyle is used to being criticized for her psychic abilities, yet the tough-as-nails—and drop-dead-gorgeous—detective has no doubt about what she has uncovered in the case of a string of unsolved murders. And Tierney is slowly discovering that working so close to her partner, detective Wade Callahan, could be lethal.

Look for

Danger Signals
by Kathleen Creighton

Available in April wherever books are sold.

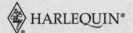

HARLEQUIN®

American ★ Romance®

COMING NEXT MONTH

#1205 RUNAWAY COWBOY by Judy Christenberry
The Lazy L Ranch
Jessica Ledbetter has worked too hard on her family's dude ranch to let
Jim Bradford, a cowboy turned power broker and the ranch's new manager,
show her up. The Lazy L is Jess's legacy, and she isn't about to let it fall into
the hands of an outsider. No matter what those hands can do to her...

#1206 MARRYING THE BOSS by Megan Kelly
When Mark Collins finds himself in a competition with Leanne Fairbanks for
the position of CEO of the family business, he can't believe it. But as they go
head-to-head in a series of tasks to fight for the top job, Mark begins to see her
as more than just a rival. And if he wins, will he lose *her?*

#1207 THE MARRIAGE RECIPE by Michele Dunaway
Catching her fiancé in bed with one of the restaurant's curvaceous employees
sends up-and-coming pastry chef Rachel Palladia fleeing Manhattan for the
comforts of home. But when her ex threatens to sue for her dessert recipes, she
turns to her high school heartthrob, Colin Morris, who happens to be the town
lawyer—and he's a lot sweeter than revenge!

#1208 DOWN HOME DIXIE by Pamela Browning
No real Southern belle would fall for a Yankee—especially not one named
Kyle Sherman. But Dixie Lee Smith does, and hides the truth about his
illustrious ancestor from her family. What's worse, as soon as she finds out
she's got competition, *she* goes to war—to keep the handsome Northerner
for herself!

www.eHarlequin.com

HARCNM0308